ACCEPTANCE

Ibitola Ojoye-Adebayo

ACCEPTANCE

Ibitola Ojoye-Adebayo

www.completelynovel.com

Biography

Ibitola Ojoye-Adebayo is a graduate of the University of Portsmouth with a BSc in Pharmacology. Sparked by a passion for gothic horror, mystery and romance novels; her top writing influences include Virginia Andrews and Stephen King. Ibitola's debut novel, *Acceptance*, is a powerful testimony of love, pain and triumph; a fire that was lit the year her first child was born and fervently written, then put aside - until the year that she got married. When Ibitola isn't raising three children with her husband, she continues to inspire and create in various online communities through her writing and research.

Acceptance by **Ibitola Ojoye-Adebayo**

Copyright © 2013 by Ibitola Ojoye-Adebayo

Printed and bound in the United Kingdom by Antony Rowe.

ISBN 9781849143875

Published by Completely Novel

www.completelynovel.com

Cover design by Kelly Van der Weide

This book is dedicated to my husband. 'Kola without you this book wouldn't be possible.'

'Darkness cannot drive out darkness: only light can do

that. Hate cannot drive out hate: only love can do that.'

— Martin Luther King, Jr

PROLOGUE:

HERCULES

Acceptance exists at the core of our being. It is our default status. In order to reach this base level of acceptance, one need only remove the items lying on top. To do this, we must first identify all the things we do not accept around us. Then, one by one, eliminate them.

This I did without so much as a backward glance or afterthought. But the people who hurt me deserved it. After today, no one will ever hurt or crush my world again.

Looking back, I would say I had always been a fighter. Never backing down to anything or anyone, never accepting being second best, and definitely never ever letting a man walk all over me or put me down. But all that changed six years ago when Richard entered my life, my love for him clouded every judgement.

He is the sole reason I am standing here in the dark, with tears like a lake, still and unflowing. I look down at the knife in my hands; I can't see it in the dark. I touch the tip with my fingers; it feels sticky to the touch. An anguished moan makes me flinch, looking over to my right; my eyes linger at the monstrosity on the floor. I blink twice, turn back to face the kitchen sink, and smile staring into the night.

The clock chimes, 5.00 pm. My heart skips a beat. This was the fateful time I met Richard, six years ago in Aberdeen.

I can't help smiling to myself in a mad and inhuman way, I can remember that day clearly like it was yesterday. It was August 1998 and I was still a fresher at the University of Aberdeen, working part time in a local supermarket. Back then I thought nothing could be better than that.

I had got into the university of my choice after much awaited A-Level results. I was finally living away from home, to my mother's dismay. She tried as hard as she could to persuade me to choose a university in London, but I put my foot down. That was one choice in my life I made sure she couldn't influence in any way. I was determined to live as far away from home as possible, away from my mother's constant disapproving 'looks and smirks'. I wanted to be free and I was loving every moment of it.

But I will leave my mother's story for a while and continue with when I first met Richard, even though the root of all my problems today is my mother. I truly believe I would not be contemplating the thought dancing in my head right now if it hadn't been for the lack of motherly love through the years.

Getting back to Richard, fresh tears start to flow once more. My first smell of him was intoxicating. You may be wondering why I choose to describe my first encounter with him as a smell. Well, because that was exactly what his presence brought with him. When he walked into a room, all you could smell was this exhilarating manly perfume that made you look up from whatever you were doing and seek out the culprit.

On this very day, in August 1998. There was a queue of customers reaching God knows where. I was so tired. Having started work at 8.00 am that morning, by 4.45 pm I was anxious to get out and I had lost concentration all together. I constantly kept looking at my wrist watch, wishing desperately that I could bend time and space. At least then I would be able to fast forward time, and to get the hell out of there. Glancing at my watch again, I sighed in dismay, only five minutes had passed since the last time I checked.

I continued serving customers with my head down. Suddenly, I was aware of the most intoxicating scent I had ever smelt in my whole life. I looked up, thinking it was the customer I was serving, but it was not because she was a woman and the scent I could smell was masculine. Putting the thought aside, I tried to serve as many customers as I could before 5.00 pm.

Subconsciously, I was getting the distinct

feeling that the scent was getting nearer

and nearer but I was not concentrating, as

my whole mission was to handover my till

at five. Suddenly my senses were

overwhelmed with the scent, and for a

minute I was almost swimming in pool of

orgasmic bliss.

I looked up and there standing before me

was Hercules himself, the biceps on him

were unbelievable. I just wanted to rip

open his shirt and stroke and stroke. I was

still staring in amazement, thinking to

myself *'what lucky bitch had this one?'*

when he smiled. *'Oh what perfect*

dimples.' I was taken to a world of

enlightenment that I had never been to before. I would have stayed there too if it wasn't for the aggressive way my arm was being poked.

Rushing back down to earth, I realised that my replacement, Sue, was prodding me in the arm and calling my name. People were beginning to stare and I felt myself going hot in the face. If I were much lighter skinned my embarrassment would have shown quite clearly. *'Thank God.'*

I apologised to Hercules and finished scanning his items.
'£25.40 please,' I said. He looked at me and gave me a lopsided smile.

'You know what?' he said, leaning forward. 'Give me your number then I'll pay.'

'You're joking right?' I said, laughing slightly.

'Nope,' he said with a chuckle. I declined gracefully but he wouldn't budge.

'I'm sorry but I don't give out my number to strangers.' Even though I was ready to give him my number, address, bra size even my panty size.

He looked at me with great disappointment then a lady behind him said, 'Hey love just give it to him you know you want to, so what's the problem?' He smiled at me with the most perfect set of teeth.

That did it for me, because the next thing I

remember, I was jotting down my number on one of the store's leaflets and thrusting it into his hands. He paid for the items and promised to call me that night.

Sue gave me a knowing look but I just smirked at her. We exchanged positions, and as I walked away I looked at my wrist watch. Realising it was 5.15pm I raced down the aisles. I was expecting my parents and, unfortunately, I hadn't prepared for their arrival, even though they had informed me three days previously that they would be coming to visit.

I was dreading the visit because I knew it would go very wrong as soon as that mother of mine stepped out of the car. She had a tendency to complain about every single thing, which bugged the hell out of me. To this day, I still don't understand why my dad didn't divorce her years ago. I know it is a bad thing to wish on one's parents, but if you knew my mother you would be saying the same thing too. I guess my dad loves her in more ways than one.

While on my bus journey back home my mind wandered back to the handsome stranger whose name was a mystery, I felt a hot flutter move from below right up to the tip of my lips and my last thought before I got off the bus was *'Hercules please call me, please.'*

I

MOTHER

My mother grew up in Nigeria. Like most other people from her tribe, she lived with her family in a remote village. In 1966, a military junta came to power in a coup, and after riots and massacres against Ibos, on 30 May 1967 the Governor of the Eastern Region, Lt. Col. Ojukwu, announced a unilateral secession of the state of Biafra. My mother fled her homeland during the Biafra war, and became one of the thousands of Nigerian people now living in the United Kingdom.

Here she met my father who had also fled

the war and I presume fell in love with him, even though you couldn't tell with my mother. They got married three years later. From as far back as I could remember, my mother had always got her own way. I used to wonder why my dad would put up with all the bullshit she threw at him day in, day out. But like I said before, I guess he loved her. I hated my mother when I was growing up, always wanting to hear a word of praise from her, and getting only rules and expectations that I could never live up to. I remembered the years she made me get up at 6.00 am every morning and cook breakfast for my sister, Janet, before leaving for school. I remembered the slumber parties, dances, and after-school sports I missed because she didn't approve. Most of all, I remembered the times she'd compared me to other girls of my age and found me lacking.

Through generations of famine, disease, and war, Ibo women had taught their daughters what they needed to survive: how to cook, clean, haul water, and manufacture textiles; how to be productive, obedient, respectful, and patient. But as a teenager growing up in the UK, I found it hard to take these lessons as evidence of love.

Snapping out of my daydream I realised that an hour had passed from the time given for their arrival, but no parents. I looked out of the window but there was no sign of them.

This was unlike my father as he was never late for anything. He was as punctual as you can get. That was definitely one trait I knew I got from him. My sister, on the other hand, was a different story. Janet was a perpetual latecomer. I remember my mother saying one day *'that sister of yours; if you give her the chance she'll be late for her own funeral.'*

I went into the kitchen to check on the cooking, I had rearranged and cleaned everything in the house that might catch my mother's all-seeing eye. Even though I was dreading the visit, deep inside I still wanted to see them. Three months had passed since I left home, before then I had never been anywhere else for longer than a week. So I guess homesickness had started to creep in. I opened the front door and looked down the street, but still there was no sign of them. I began to get quite worried; I picked up my phone and dialed my father's mobile. But there was no answer. I didn't bother with my mother because she refused to have a mobile phone even though I had offered to buy her one.

After waiting for what seemed like eternity I called Janet, who confirmed that they had left as planned. Suddenly, the doorbell rang, a flood of relief swept over me. I hurriedly said goodbye to my sister and went to the front door.

'Hi mum, hi dad,' I said excitedly as I

hugged them.

'Hello love,' my father replied giving me

a great big hug. I looked over at

my mother who by this time was making

her way into the lounge.

I sighed and looked at my father. 'So why

are you guys so late?' I asked. 'You were

supposed to be here an hour ago.' I

noticed a slight frown on my father's face,

but it disappeared as quickly as it came.

'Sorry about that love, we got stuck in

traffic,' he said with a wary smile.

'But you could have called dad!' He

apologised again and I hugged him.

'What's wrong with mum?' I asked.

'Nothing!' She is just in one of her moods,

just let her be for now.'

That was my dad, he had never complained about my mum not even once in front of me. I'd always hope to meet somebody who would meet the same expectations as my dad.

I took my dad to the lounge. 'Here dad relax, I'll get you a cold drink.'

'Thanks love,' he said as he settled down on the sofa. Leaving him to unwind, I approached the kitchen, and what I saw didn't surprise me one bit. I could see my mother dust testing every spot in there. I rolled my eyes and walked in as she was making her way to the fridge.

'Hey, mum, are you OK?' She mumbled something I couldn't quite catch. 'Mum, are you OK?' I asked her again.

'What did your father say to you?' she said abruptly, moving away from the fridge and starting to inspect the oven.

'Oh, nothing much, just that you guys were stuck in traffic,' I said nonchalantly. I was trying very hard not to give her the reaction she wanted.

'Is that so?' she made a sound in between a laugh and a grunt.

'Mum, are you alright,' I asked again. I was getting tired of playing the same old mind games with her. She stopped peering in the oven and turned around to look at me. There was an emptiness in her gaze that had no end.

'We had a quarrel,' she said with disdain.

'What about?' I asked knowing very well I shouldn't have.

A sudden spark ignited in her eyes and she started screaming. 'Do you know what that man out there said to me?' Her outburst didn't surprise me, because that was my mother through and through.

'Calm down mum, just tell me what happened?'

'Calm down?' she snapped at me with contempt. 'Don't tell me to calm down.'

At that moment my father walked into the kitchen, which was a big mistake.

'Is everything alright Eva?' he asked with concern.

'Yes dad!' I noticed my mother giving my dad a look that would kill a newborn baby rabbit. 'Mum whatever dad said I'm sure he didn't mean it.' I said with a smile

trying to reassure her, but it didn't work.

'Didn't mean it?' she replied with a snarl.

'What do you know anyway, it's not as if

you're old enough to know the meaning of

life?'

That did it. I was tired of my mother

treating me like a child, it was about time

she realised that I was not a little girl who

she could control at will.

'Mum, I know you're upset at the moment

but you must understand you are no longer

speaking to a child. I am sick and tired of

you putting me down as if my words,

views or thoughts don't count for

anything,' I said scornfully. 'I am bloody

21 now, if you don't know.' By the time I

realised was I was doing I was shouting at her and it was too late, but she knew how to press my buttons. I realised that my father would be the one to get the edge of her tongue, and I was right, she looked at me for a few seconds blinking rapidly, and without a word she turned on my father.

'You see Samson,' my mother screamed at him. 'You've turned her against me, I hope you're satisfied.' And with that, she pushed past us sniffing uncontrollably, went straight into my bedroom and slammed the door behind her. Thank God my housemate and best friend, J, wasn't in I would have died of *SHAME*.

My father came over and hugged me.

'Don't worry love, she is just in a crappy

mood, you know she can't help being a drama queen,' he said, patting me gently on the cheeks. My face was as hot as a fire cracker.

'Nothing for your pretty head to worry about,' he said with a low chuckle. That was my dad always the optimist.

'OK, but go and talk to her before she rips my room apart.'

He went over to my bedroom door, but it was bolted from within.

'Open up, Abigail.' She didn't answer.

'Open up now,' he said the second time but still she didn't answer him. 'Abi, don't make me break this door down.' That seemed to work because my mother unbolted the door. My dad winked at me and went in shutting the door behind him.

I left them to it.

They were in there for a while. When eventually they did come out, my mother's face was so flushed that I had to do a double take. I tried to catch her eye but she kept her gaze down and walked past me into the kitchen. But as she passed I definitely saw a hint of a smile at the corner of her lips. Sudden realisation dawned on me. *'Yuck.'* I was definitely changing my sheets when they left.

We had lunch without any more dramas. I got compliments on my meal from my father but my mother only picked at her food.

'You could have done with a bit of seasoning in the soup, haven't I taught you anything?' she said with a slight irritation in her voice. I stared back at her expressionless.

'You see Samson if you hadn't allowed her to move down to this God forsaken city she would have learned how to prepare some home cooked meals and be able to clean more efficiently,' she said to my father, looking at me without blinking. 'What husband will marry her if she can't do any of those essential things, I tell you Samson it was a big mistake letting her come here,' she said matter-of-factly.

My dad just smiled back at her like a smitten puppy. I, however, was fuming like a volcano ready to erupt; she was definitely getting on my nerves. But I calmed down because I knew they were only staying for the night. They were leaving for London the next day. *'Thank God.'* And as soon as they left my sheets went straight into the washer.

II

RICHARD

It was Friday, two days after my path crossed with Hercules. I had completely forgotten about him. I was waiting at the bus stop when my mobile phone rang.

'Hello?' I said down the line.

'Hi, Eva.'

'Who is this?'

'It's Richard.'

'Who?' I asked knowing perfectly well it was him. My Hercules.

'You know, the guy you gave your number to at the supermarket.'

'Oh hi, Richard, how are you?' I asked trying to act nonchalantly.

'I'm fine, just wanted to know if we could meet up this evening?'

'Erm, what time?'

'Would 8 o'clock be OK?' he asked.

'Sure, see you then. Bye.'

'Hold up, Eva.'

'Yea!'

'You haven't given me your address.'

'Oops sorry.' I gave it out to him and we said our goodbyes. I lingered on the phone for a while trying to capture his scent but nothing. I realised then, that I didn't have an outfit to wear for my date with my Greek demi-god.

From the bus stop, I headed towards the shopping centre on the other side of the road. I had to get something really slick. As I walked into the shopping centre I dialed J's number, he was my best friend and housemate. He had made a bet with me that he would be getting a date first that summer.

Five hours later I was getting ready for, what turned out to be, the most exciting date I'd ever been on. As I was getting ready, J kept asking me questions about my new found hunk through my closed bedroom door. I tried to answer his many questions. I was quite used to him buzzing around me. As we were talking, I slipped into my dress. Then the doorbell rang.

'I'll get it, you just get dressed,' he screamed as he rushed downstairs. Five minutes later J came back to my door.

'Hey, Eva, lover boy is here. Are you

ready?' he asked.

'Yes come in,' I yelled. As J walked in I twirled around. 'So how do I look?' I asked him eagerly, I had always respected his opinion. He let out a slight gasp, 'Eva you look stunning.'

'Are you sure, it doesn't look too sluttish or desperate?'

'No, you've even got my heart racing and I'm not your date.'

'Shut up J,' I said, hitting him playfully. Picking up my purse I took one final look in the mirror and went downstairs.

Waving to J as he closed the front door, I got into Richard's car. Richard got into the driver's seat.

'You look more beautiful than I remember,' Richard said as we drove off.

'So where too?' I asked trying to act cool. He looked exquisite in his black suit.

'There's this lovely place near Crown Terrace that I thought you might like,' he said with a broad smile.

'That's cool with me,' I said trying very hard to keep my eyes ahead. Just his mere presence sent my body tingling. We arrived at the restaurant 30 minutes later, by then my hands where sweating so badly I had to keep wiping them with my hanky. I had never been this nervous and unresponsive in all my life I was usually the chatterbox. I felt like such a fool.

We entered the restaurant and were

ushered to our seats. The restaurant was
enchanting and mesmerizing. I felt as if I
had just walked onto a movie set, I
suddenly became very self-conscious and
underdressed. Richard, sensing my
hesitation, reassured me with a slight rub
on the arm. This made heat waves shoot
up my arm causing me too jerk
backwards. Richard looked at me with a
worried expression.

'Eva, are you alright?'

'Yes, it's just a bit chilly in here' I said as
I pretended to shiver slightly.

'Would you like my jacket?' he offered.

'No thanks, I'm OK' I said with a smile.

He squeezed my hands.

'Would you be up for dancing after our
meal? It might help to relax you because

you look too tense.' Reclaiming my hands I agreed.

I'd wished that he would stop touching me, it was driving me crazy, and causing all my senses to malfunction. If my mum could have seen me she would have slapped the shamelessness out of me.

As we ate and talked I studied him covertly. He had smooth, wavy, short dark hair, was quite tall and very well built, I found it hard to tell how old he was he was; somewhere between 29 and 35 I guessed. Having exchanged enough information about each other to fill a book, I realised how easy it was to talk to him. Richard was neither a clown nor a joke-teller but he was a funny guy with razor sharp observations and the ability to see humor in everything and everyone. The club wasn't that bad either. We danced and danced. Near the end of the night Richard requested a song from the DJ. He pulled me to the middle of the dance floor and Whitney Houston's *'I will always love you'* came bouncing off the speakers. I was shocked as this was one of my all-time favourite hits.

I couldn't resist resting my head on his broad shoulders and as we moved to the music his hands went up and down my back. This awakened a desire deep within my heart that I had never felt before. I'd had other boyfriends but none had awoken anything in me the way that Richard did then. My legs buckled below me and I stepped back.

'It's getting late can we go now?' I asked without looking at him. He stood there watching me with a funny expression on his face.

'OK, if you want.'

Arriving at my doorstep 45 minutes later, I turned round and faced Richard.

'I had a lovely time tonight, thank you.'

'You're welcome; I hope we can do it again soon,' he said stepping back. I turned round and opened the front door, but something was telling me not to be a fool; to invite him in.

'Richard.'

'Yes,' he said with a smile.

'Would you like to come in for a cuppa?' I felt nervous because I had never done this before especially on a first date. This was a bold move on my part, which my friends would have called risky. But all my inhibitions went out of the window.

'Sure. I'll love to,' he said, following me inside.

After three cups of coffee and a tour through my family album, Richard looked at his watch.

'Eva I've got to go, it's five in the morning!' he exclaimed.

'Is it, I didn't realise?' I said not caring very much, I was having a wonderful time.

He stood up to give me a hug and as he

moved to kiss my cheeks, our lips met and

I couldn't stop myself - we kissed

passionately. I could see the desire in his

eyes and he could see mine.

'Eva, ever since I saw you I wanted you. I

haven't felt this way about anybody for a

long time,' he said pulling me closer. 'I

had to muster all my strength just to call

you hoping to God you wouldn't say no.'

That was it, I melted in his arms. He kept

saying my name over and over again,

which sounded somewhere between a sigh

and a groan. He kissed my neck, my eyes,

my breasts, returning hungrily to my lips

for more. His hands ran over my body,

teasing me. He ripped open my blouse, my

buttons flew everywhere. My

subconscious was telling me to stop but I

couldn't - I was gone. I ripped open his shirt and led him to my bedroom. As we approached the bed his eyes were questioning as he lay down beside me. The slight nod of my head reassured him it was what I wanted. I wrapped my arms around him holding him close so that he would not see the fear in my eyes. The warmth of his body against mine and the neat fit of him inside me made my body ripple with double orgasmic pleasure. I could feel no pain.

When we finished we lay there holding each other. I started to wiggle as he stroked my nipples, then he whispered my name. I looked up at him and smiled. 'You should have told me you were a virgin.' I stiffened, shame flowing over me.

'Oh baby, come here.' He held me close for a very long while. Then he whispered in my ear. 'Eva, you don't need to be ashamed, I am here to stay.'

'You're just saying that, I might not see you for dust come tomorrow.'

'You're wrong Eva, I've been waiting for you all my life and now that I've found you I refuse to let you go.' I looked into his eyes and I couldn't stop my tears from flowing.

'Do you really mean it?' I said pressing up against him.

'Yes Eva, will you be my girl?'

'Oh yes, Richard, I'll love to be your girl.'

With those last words we fell asleep

holding each other like two Siamese

twins.

III

GRADUATION

My graduation day went off with a bang. I didn't get a first-class honours like my parents wanted but a 2:1 was good all the same. At the end of the ceremony I approached my parents excitedly.

'Oh Eva, I'm so proud of you,' my dad said as he hugged me. I looked over at my mother and I swear I saw a hint of pride in her eyes but within seconds it had disappeared.

'Why couldn't you have got a first class like that Asian boy in your year?' she mumbled.

'Abi!' my dad scolded at her. Ignoring her

I scanned the crowd for Richard and noticing him standing not too far away, I turned to my parents.

'Mum, dad.'

'Yes', they answered simultaneously. I gulped and letting out a deep breath I opened my mouth.

'Apart from J somebody else will be joining us for lunch, is that OK?'

'Who?' my mother asked. I beckoned to Richard to come over.

'Mum, dad, I'd like you to meet my friend Richard,' I announced as I pulled him towards them. 'Richard, these are my parents.' My father shook Richard's outstretched hand.

'It's lovely to finally meet you sir.' Turning to my mother, he bowed slightly, 'and you Madam.'

And without as much as an expression my mother nodded.

After the pleasantries we all made our way to the hall for the graduation lunch; the hall had been superbly decorated by me and a few other graduation committee members.

As we sat down at our table J came over, he hugged my dad and kissed my mum on the cheek, nodded at Richard and sat down. His parents couldn't make it to the graduation due to his mum falling ill. I didn't know the extent of the illness then, only that she had collapsed. I gave him a smile and he grinned at me in a mischievous way. My mother asked J how his mother was doing and if she was taking her medication that she had picked up for her at the pharmacy the day before. J replied that she was and by the time he had left her place that morning she was brightening up. That brought a smile to my mother's face and she nodded in understanding.

During the meal I noticed that my mother hadn't said much, which was unlike her. She always complained about everything no matter where we were. She complained about the food, the service, the setting of cutlery on the table, even the décor. I looked at her and she was shooting daggers at my dad with her eyes. I glanced at dad but he seemed to be oblivious to her looks. He was busy chatting away with Richard and J about football.

Looking over at my mother, our eyes met and I smiled at her but all I got back was a slight grinding of her teeth. The venomous way in which she did it made me nearly choke on the chicken I was eating. Coughing, I stood up.

'Where are you going?' Richard asked pulling me back down.

'I'll be right back, I just need to go to the ladies.' I felt horrible leaving him there but I just had to get away. In the cloakroom, I splashed water on my face and wiped it. Checking for an empty cubicle I entered, locked the door behind me and sat down. I dipped my hand in my right pocket and brought out the engagement ring Richard had given me three weeks earlier. Looking at it caused warm feelings to wash over me. We had been together for three years now, we'd had our ups and downs like any other couple, but when he proposed I was still shocked.

My mind wandered back to that day, it was my birthday and Richard had arranged to cook something special for me at his place. I was excited because Richard never cooked, he didn't know how to. For him to learn just for me was very special indeed.

Sitting around a candlelit table, we had just finished eating a very delicious meal when Richard stood up to clear away the dishes. When he returned, he poured me another glass of Champagne. He pulled his seat closer to mine, held my hands and kissed me and, as always, I became immediately aroused. I could taste the red wine he'd been drinking.

'Hmmm,' I moaned.

Richard looked at me for what seemed like forever. 'Richard what is it?' I asked.

'Eva.'

'Yes.'

'You know I will always love you even if you don't end up being mine forever?'

I looked at him puzzled, wondering why he would ask such a question. He turned my chair round so that we were face-to-face and then he knelt down on one knee.

I flinched.

And with my hands in his, he looked up at me with those piercing eyes of his and smiled. I started to shake uncontrollably. Richard, what are you doing?' I asked with quivering lips.

'Eva, ever since I met you I knew you were the one for me,' he said softly. 'I don't care about any other girls, I know there were times when I've hurt you and it's caused a strain in the relationship, but you've never complained or threatened to leave.' I shifted uncomfortably in my seat. 'Richard,' I said nearly choking. But he stopped me by placing a finger on my lips. 'I really appreciate you sticking by me and loving me. I don't want to be alone anymore, I wake up at night sometimes screaming your name but you're never there.' He paused and wiped the tear that was threatening to release itself from my eyes then continued, 'I don't think I can go through another night without you beside me, waking up with me, eating with me, sleeping with and holding me.' By now I was sniffing uncontrollably.

'Eva.'

'Yes,' I whimpered.

'Will you marry me?

'Yes, oh yes, Richard,' I squealed. With that he brought out the most breathtaking engagement ring I had ever seen. He placed it in my finger and I couldn't help but stare at it. 'Richard?'

'Yes?'

'I love you with all my heart and soul.

Thank you for making me whole,' I said,
my eyes swimming with tears.

His hand slid up my dress groping for my
bra fastening. I found myself arching
against him, wanting the thrill of his
touch.

'Richard,' I moaned.

'I can't think about anything else but
touching you Eva', he said with a sigh. He
started to peel off my clothes. Richard's
touch was thrilling, exciting, sensitive,
gentle and so sensual that I found myself
moaning with pleasure. There was a
moment where I felt a stab of jealousy,
towards all the other women he'd
pleasured before. But that moment passed;
for how could I be angry about what he
had done with other women when what

mattered was that he was here, right now with me. By the time he entered me, I was transported to the highest Alps. I was in ecstasy.

After making love we cuddled up for a while. I got up to get Richard a glass of water and as I watched him drink it an idea popped into my head. 'Richard you know what?' I said excitedly.

'What?' he asked looking up at me.

'I would like to tell my parents about our engagement on my graduation day.

'Are you sure that's not too soon?' he asked looking concerned.

'Richard, trust me, the sooner my parents know the easier it will be for my mother to absorb it.

'OK, if that's what you want, let's do it. Don't worry, I'll be on my best behaviour,' he said with a smirk.

'It's settled then.'

'Will your father ask me if my intentions towards you are honorable? he said, chuckling.

'Of course he will, he's an African man after all. But you're lucky he's much more easygoing than my mother.' Richard leaned forward and kissed me, sending chills up my thigh. I held his face in my hands, kissed his generous sexy lips and his chocolate-brown skin. I smiled at him feeling fulfilled and satisfied from within - we were like twin souls entwined together forever. His love was all I wanted. Richard, sensing my desire, pulled me on top of him.

'Eva, I love you, and want to look after you for the rest of my life,' he said as he stroked my bottom.

'Let's see what tomorrow brings first,' I whispered. 'You might change your mind when you finally meet my mother.'

IV

THE NEWS

I was still daydreaming when I heard a knock on my cubicle. 'Sorry, I'll be out in a minute.' I put the ring back in my pocket and stepped out, it was do or die.

Reaching the table, I noticed that my mother was still in the same mode that I had left her in *'Mute.'* I sat down and Richard reached for my hand under the table and squeezed.

I drank some water and looked round the table. My father was exactly what everyone expected from a Professor of Physics: tall and thin with stooping shoulders, glasses slightly askew on his nose, and a wide expanse of forehead which grew larger every year as his black hair receded even further. Despite having a very strong bond with my father, I didn't appear to have inherited any of his looks but fortunately, I had inherited his keen intelligence. Unfortunately, I look more like my mother, but the similarities end there.

Looking over at her I sighed, she was poised like a graceful, but ever watchful deer. She looked beautiful in her cream three piece suit and pearls, with her braids wrapped up in a neat chignon, but the effect was spoiled by a fixed false smile. My mouth tasted as if I'd eaten chalk. I steadied myself and began, 'Mum, dad.' I looked at both of them. 'I've got something to tell you.'

'What is it Eva?' My dad said with a smile. My mother, on the other hand, turned slightly in her seat and stared at me full on. I gulped and continued.

'Richard has asked me to marry him, and I've accepted.' There was a sharp intake of breath from my mother, then silence. My dad looked at Richard for what seemed like an age, and then he spoke.

'Young man is this true?'

'Yes, Mr. Hamilton,' Richard said with a smile. 'We've been dating for three years now, and I love your daughter very much. I would like to ask for her hand in marriage.' My father nodded as he normally did when he was deep in thought.

'You know Richard, this has not come as

a surprise. Eva is my baby, and she was brought up properly. She wouldn't have introduced you today if your relationship wasn't serious.' He paused and looked over at my mother. 'We love her and want to make her happy, so we accept on one condition, that we get to know you a bit better before you marry her. Is that alright with you?'

'Yes sir,' he said as he squeezed my hands under the table. I smiled and got up to give my dad a hug. But my mother stood up nearly knocking her seat over.

'We accept?' she spat. 'Samson when did you start speaking for me or making decisions for us without consulting me first, aren't I your wife after all?'

My father gave her a cold look and said

sternly, 'Abigail sit down and don't make a scene.'

My mother ignored him and looked at me. 'You've made your bed, now you can lie in it,' she snapped. 'Don't come crying to us when he deserts you for some common trollop more suited to him,' she said with disdain. She picked up her purse and glared at my father, 'Samson take me back to the hotel I don't feel well.'

'Abigail, why are you getting yourself so worked up?' my father asked. My mother went pale.

'Samson,' she said, very slowly, spitting it out with venom. 'If you don't take me back to the hotel now there will be hell to pay.'

My father's eyes narrowed behind his

glasses. Standing up, he walked over to me and kissed me softly on the cheek.

'Eva, we'll see you back in London. My dad said at the same time he looking angrily over at my mother.

'OK, dad, take care,' I replied hugging him. My mother didn't say a word. I tried to catch her eye but she refused to look me in the face. I felt a wave of anger begin to make its way slowly up from my stomach to my throat. I swallowed it down, and held back.

As they left I felt suddenly strange and faint, on the edge of some mental and emotional overload. Tears rolled down my eyes and as I sat back down I noticed J was standing up. He walked over to me and gave me a tight hug.

'Don't worry Eva, things will be alright. You know how your mother can get, just take her words like a pinch of salt.' I looked up and smiled, hugging him tighter.

'Thanks J,' I said, sniffing. I noticed him looking at Richard, the look in his eyes was haunting. I knew J wasn't too keen on my relationship with Richard. They just didn't get along from the start which I just couldn't understand. I sometimes noticed J giving Richard cold looks when he thought nobody could see him. From the time Richard and I started to get serious I noticed J was slipping away from me. I tried speaking to him about it but he just brushed it off. A friend of mine had told me one time that J had had a crush on me since high school but I was too blind to see. I didn't believe this because J had always treated me like a sister. I didn't believe he could have such feelings for me. He gave me one final hug, excused himself and left.

When Richard and I got back to the car, I cried and cried.

'Don't cry Eva, please don't cry. I love you,' he said, as he cradled me in his arms. 'I can't bear to see you so upset,' he said as he kissed my tears away.

'It's just that it's turned out so awful Richard!' My mother had that look in her eyes as if I'd let her down in some way.'

'Don't worry, Eva, just give your mum

time,' he said as he held me close, kissing both eyes.

'Do you love me?' he asked lifting my head up.

'You know I do, but after what you've seen and heard today I'm surprised you still want to marry me?'

He tenderly took off my glasses and wiped away a tear that was threatening to drop once again.

'Eva, you know I do, if we stick by each other everything will be alright.'

My frown slowly melted away and I smiled a little. 'Yes. I know you do. And I will stick by you no matter what.'

He held me for a very long while, eventually I dozed off and he drove me home.

V

$HOME$

When I got back to London after three
years of studying in Aberdeen, I didn't
recognise the place, everything seemed so
new, and people were busy rushing
around. At home I tried hard to treat my
mother's attitude in the same way as
Richard and my father did, but I couldn't.
I felt so angry and indignant that she
didn't even give him a chance.

It was becoming intolerable at home.
There was no let-up in my mother's digs
about Richard. Most of the time I
managed to ignore her, but every now and
then I would retaliate and it would turn

into a full-scale argument. Each time it happened I was shocked at my mother's venom, anyone overhearing her would assume Richard was the devil himself. After three months being back home in London and my mother and father's constant bickering, my father called me into their bedroom. Upon entering I saw my mother sitting on the bed. Hesitating at the door I looked over at my father, questioning him with my eyes. But he ushered me in impatiently.

'Eva, come in we haven't got all day.'

'Sorry dad,' I said as I made my way over to my mother's dressing table and sat down on a chair. My father began.

'Your mother and I have been talking and we have reached a common ground.' I sat up straight in my seat. 'You'll have to forgive your mother for her behaviour for the past couple of months, but you should understand that you did spring this on her unexpectedly.' I looked over at my mother but she kept her head down. 'Eva, your mother has agreed to give her blessing to the wedding.' I gave my dad a questioning look.

'What's the catch?' I said with annoyance.

'Eva, don't be cocky,' my dad said sternly.

'Sorry,' I mumbled. 'Why?' I asked sounding honestly surprised. I looked over at my dad uncertainly, then back at my mother. Her eyes shifted, and when I followed them I felt a surge of dread. My mother stood up and started pacing the room, eventually stopping at the window looking out at something far beyond the horizon I guess only she could see. Eventually she turned round.

'Evelyn, come over here.' I looked at my dad hesitantly. My mother only ever called me by that name when she was really pissed at me. 'Evelyn?' she repeated.

'Yes mum,' I said curiously, walking over to her.

As I reached my mother she drew closer and reached out to me with a hand that felt numb. She grasped my hands and I stiffened. My mother had never shown any kind of physical contact towards either one of her daughters in my entire existence, so this action scared me. 'Eva,' she said as she squeezed my fingers. I know I might come across as harsh sometimes but it's for your own good.' A tear rolled down my mother's left cheek. 'I just want you to have a better life as a young woman than I ever had, if I had a mother to steer me in the right direction, I wouldn't have made some of the drastic decisions I made along the way,' she paused and squeezed my fingers again before continuing. 'But I thank God I made some right ones,' she said looking over at my father and as he stared back at her, an unspoken understanding passed between them.

'So what are you saying mum?' I asked, partly confused and partly scared of what was coming next.

'As you know your grandmother died when I was quite young and having a stepmother who was bent in making my life a misery to look after me, I ended up fending for myself.' She blinked away a tear that was threatening to fall. 'I've accepted you marrying Richard solely because I can see you love him very much and he is able to look after you financially. Regardless of what you think of me, your happiness has always come first.' I looked at my mother for the weirdest 20 seconds and hugged her deeply.

'Thank you mum, I love you.' She smiled and hugged me back. I walked over to my father to give him a well-deserved hug, but my mother stopped me in my tracks.

'Keep in mind, Evelyn, just because I have consented to this marriage it doesn't mean I like Richard any more than I already do. There is something about that boy I don't trust and that's that.' I looked at my dad and just smiled. I didn't really care about her feelings towards Richard, all I cared about was that she had given her blessing and I was getting married.

Three months later, Richard and I got married and I was encased in marital bliss - until everything started to fall apart. When they did, Richard, who was supposed to be my light at the end of the darkest tunnel to guide me home, wasn't there. All I found was PAIN and SUFFERING that knew no end.

VI

MARITAL BLISS

Our wedding day went off without any hitches. Richard and I had agreed to recite our own wedding vows. My mother took over everything, even to the extent of choosing the colour of my bouquet. But funnily enough I didn't mind. My mother is a lot of things but seeing the passion and zest in her eyes; I felt that if I complained I would be ripping away a long awaited dream. Like I said before, my mother didn't have much of a childhood and she was brought up to fend for herself. She was forced to be smart and witty to get through various obstacles in her life and this, I believed, caused her to grow up into a bitter woman. Those parts of her life I had grown to understand and accept. My mother had agreed to be civil to Richard and his family, especially his mum, whom she hated with a passion. Please don't ask me why.

At the reception I scanned the guests for J, but he wasn't there. This made me agitated. J was supposed to be there, he had promised me. I had forgiven him for not being able to attend my engagement party due to a family emergency he had to deal with back in the States. His step-sister who lived over there with her husband had gotten into a car accident and she was in a bad way. But having promised me he would make it back in time to be at my wedding, I was certainly expecting him to be there. J was my best friend; the day wouldn't have been complete without him.

When J found out about the engagement he wasn't too happy. I had a feeling that he'd been avoiding me for some time now. It started right after I told him that Richard had proposed.

We were in his kitchen when I told him.

He went as white as a sheet.

'What?' he said in a squeaky voice.

'Richard proposed to me,' I repeated. He stared at me for a moment, then he walked towards me and sat down on one of the kitchen stools. 'J, what's wrong? Aren't you happy for me?' I asked. I was very concerned about his reaction to my news. I was expecting him to hug and congratulate me as best friends do. But he was just staring at the wall in a daze. 'J, why aren't you saying anything,' I asked, approaching him. Pulling up a stool I sat down opposite him.

'J?' I said softly. He didn't answer. 'J?' I repeated, a bit harshly, getting irritated. He finally looked at me with the oddest expression. 'When did he propose Eva?'

'Three days ago.'

Three days ago,' he repeated closing his eyes. Taking a deep breath, I stood up.

'J, you're worrying me. I know you and Richard never hit it off as much as I would have liked but you still got along with him alright so what's the problem?'

He immediately stood up. 'Oh Eva, I'm so sorry, this just took me by surprise. With all your break-ups and make-ups for the past three years I didn't think it would end up being this serious.

Relieved, I went over to hug him. 'You got me worried then old friend.' He smiled and hugged me back.

'So, how are we celebrating your big news, Eva?'

'Well, the girls are taking me to this new male strip club at Grove Square.

'Which one's that?'

'THE TWILGHT!'

'Oh you dirty girl.'

As we left his flat that day, I still felt a tingling sensation at the back of my mind

telling me that something was wrong. But
I pushed the thought away.

J was my best friend and he was the first
and the last person I could count on, apart
from Richard, to look after me and protect
me. If anything serious was wrong he
would tell me. Or, so I thought.

Richard, noticing my worried expression
and the way I was constantly scanning our
guests, pulled me towards him.

'Eva love, what's wrong?' he said,
stroking my hair.

'Nothing,' I said, still scanning the crowd.

'Are you sure?'

'Well, it's just that, J promised to be here,
but I can't seem to see him anywhere.'

Richard stopped stroking my hair and

turned me round to face him.

'I've told you to stop worrying about J, he is a big boy and if he promised to be here he will, he is your best friend after all. And moreover the day is still young; he could be making his way here from the airport right now.' I stared over at the guests once more.

'I really hope so; if he doesn't make it I'll never forgive him.'

An hour before the end of the reception Richard and I bid farewell to our guests and we made our way to the limousine. We had to get to the airport by ten because our flight left at midnight. Richard had booked a two week first class, romantic break in the Caribbean for our honeymoon. As we approached the limo I noticed J standing across the street. Without thinking I ran towards him.

'J, you made it,' I screamed. He caught me as I flung myself at him.

'Hello, Eva,' he said. 'I told you I wouldn't miss your day for the world, my flight was delayed.'

'It doesn't matter, you're here now even though the wedding is over,' I said hugging him again.

'You look absolutely beautiful Eva.'

'I know,' I said with a giggle. Then suddenly his expression changed to something unreadable.

'I think your husband is missing you already.' I glanced behind me and saw Richard making his way towards us. I turned my attention back to J.

'Are you OK?'

'Why wouldn't I be?' he said with a smile that didn't quite reach his eyes.

'J, I know there is something you're not telling me, because I can see it in your eyes. We hardly ever talk anymore.' I noticed J take a step back and shove his hands in his trouser pockets. Promise me that when I get back we will talk.' I said. With a haunting expression he replied, 'Yes, Eva. We'll talk.' He was seriously worrying me now but before I could question him any further Richard stepped up behind me, leaned down, wrapped his hands around my neck, and kissed the top of my head. I looked up at him and smiled.

'Hello Gorgeous, we are going to miss our flight,' he said, smiling faintly and nodding at J.

'Sweetie, you're going to have to forgive me but we've got a flight to catch, hope you don't mind me leaving you.' He smiled, this time focusing on everything around him but me.

'Don't worry about me go enjoy your honeymoon.' He smiled again, but with less conviction than before. I kissed him on the cheek and felt his body stiffen to my touch. I sighed quietly and let go. I said goodbye to him one last time, all the while questioning him with my eyes. But there was nothing, his eyes were dead. As Richard led me away to our waiting limo I looked back at J. I thought I saw a tear in his deep brown eyes but it was gone as soon as it came.

As we drove off in the limo I waved to J, but he didn't wave back he just stood there and watched us leave. *'He must not have seen me,'* I said to myself.

'What?' Richard asked.

'Nothing.' And as I looked back again, J was gone. I sat in deep thought all the way to the airport. As our plane flew out of Heathrow airport I snuggled closer to Richard. He held me close and kissed my forehead. As I started to drift off into a state of slumber my mind replayed the day's events. My dad wasn't that much of a softy by heart. But through the course of the day I saw him dab his eyes several times with his hanky. My mother, on the

other hand, was a different story. Not one

tear fell; she was as dry as a nun's gusset.

I smiled to myself and closed my eyes, for

as far as I was concerned my mother

didn't rule me anymore because I was

now MRS EVELYN ABIGAIL

HAASTRUP.

VII

$HONEYMOON$

When we arrived at our hotel room I was taken aback, Richard had made prior arrangements with the hotel management to decorate our room. Pink and red rose petals were sprinkled everywhere, and on the bed lay a single white rose. Beside it was a Victoria's Secret lace halter neck sleepsuit. I picked it up and ran it through my fingers it was beautiful.

Richard approached me from behind and whispered in my ear. 'Do you like it?'
'Yes, it's beautiful. 'I squeaked as Richard spanked my bottom. I span round letting

the sleepwear fall to the floor and pulled him towards me.

'Oh Richard you bring out my bad side when you do this.'

'I know, you horny minx.' And he bit my earlobe.

'Stop that Richard, you know how horny that makes me feel.'

'That's the whole point, baby.' I pushed him to arm's length. 'Richard we both stink of sweat from our journey let me run us a bath so we can soak ourselves in it and have a really naughty time.'

'Sounds good to me, you get ready while I make a few phone calls.'

'Why?'

'Don't you want the family to know we got here safely?'

'OK, but make it quick, you know how I hate to be kept waiting.' I winked and spanked his bottom. Entering the bathroom, I noticed they had quite a variety of treats on offer. There were different coloured scented candles, bath foam, scented petals, aromatic massage oils, sweets and much more. I lit one of the white candles, which smelled like apple blossom, and ran the bath. I poured in the bath foam and sprinkled red rose petals into it. When this was done I slowly peeled off my clothes and, catching my reflection in the mirror, I giggled. I was getting extremely aroused; Richard knew how to bring out my dark side. I slipped out of my bra and panties, and into the water, which was warm to the touch.

I picked up the rack of massage oils and selected my favorite Ylang Ylang because the aroma it released was deeply relaxing, exotic and sensuous. The first time Richard used it on me I came three times. I looked at the wall clock. It was midday. I realised that Richard had been gone for 20 minutes. I stepped out of the bathtub and reached for a bathrobe. Putting it on, I called out to Richard but there was no answer. I walked into the room but he wasn't there then I noticed him standing outside on the balcony. I smiled and went over to the sliding door that lead out to the balcony. I could hear him shouting at someone down the line.

'...*Why are you doing this. I told you*

before it wouldn't have worked.'

I smiled to myself thinking then, that he must have been talking to Paul. Paul was his best friend and business partner. They bickered like an old married couple. There had been many a time when I'd walked in on him and he would be pacing the room in anger and when I'd asked him what was wrong he just huffed and muttered 'It's just Paul getting on my nerves.' I'd never met Paul, as he was based in the states, but I had developed a picture of what he looked like in my mind.

As I slid open the door Richard spun round and nearly dropped his phone over the edge.

'Oh! Eva, you startled me.'

I laughed finding his facial expression hilarious. 'Why so jumpy babes, are you making plans with your mistress already?'

He looked at me and frowned. 'What's that supposed to mean?'

'Why so serious Richard, I was only joking.' He shoved his phone in his back pocket and came over to me.

'Eva, you should know you are the one I've only ever wanted.'

'I know, you keep telling me,' I said with a smile. He pulled open my robe and kissed my left breast.

'You taste so good, Eva.' I led him back into the bathroom and peeled off his clothes, kissing every inch of him. Richard lifted me up and placed me into the bathtub and then got in himself. Sitting down he pulled me towards him and I snuggled up against him, placing myself in between his legs. Picking up the Ylang Ylang Richard started to massage my nipples. I couldn't resist groaning in pleasure.

'Oh Richard,' I moaned.

'Yes darling?'

'Please, oh please Richard.'

'I know baby, I know what you want.'

Richard turned me round and took me then and there. After three rounds of explosive lovemaking I had come three times and Richard twice. He had gone, round after round like an athlete on steroids, it was unbelievable.

Having worn ourselves out we decided to go to bed. As soon as Richard's head hit the pillow, he went out like a light. I smiled to myself, I was still tingling with sensation so that I found it hard to settle down. But 30 minutes later I fell into a deep sleep.

When we got back to London, life couldn't have been any better, I was in heaven. Richard treated me like a Queen, and I loved it. One day Richard ran into the flat calling out my name. He was so excited, that he was grinning like that annoying cat in *Alice in Wonderland*.
'God I hated that film.'
'Eva put on your shoes I've got something to show you.'

'What is it?' I asked puzzled.

'Just come on.' I hurriedly slipped on my sneakers and followed him to the car. He drove for about 30 minutes and we ended up at the wealthy side of town. He parked his car and he got out to open my side of the door. I looked around confused. 'What are we doing here?'

'Just follow me, it's a surprise.' He pulled me towards him and covered my eyes with his hands. Steering me round he told me to keep walking.

'Richard, what is it?' I said laughing.

'Eva, you're so impatient we're nearly there.' Suddenly, we stopped. As he removed his hands I looked round, we were standing in front of the most exquisite house, it had a very large garage, and an enormous lawn.

'Why are we here?' I asked Richard with trembling lips.

'It's time to show you your new home,' he said and he lifted me up and carried me into the house. I couldn't believe it. The inside was unbelievable and Richard had completely furnished the whole house.

'This is all for you Eva and our future,' he said, rubbing my tummy playfully. I jokingly shoved his hands away.

'You know there's nothing happening in that department yet.'

'I know! But I can't wait to see a little me or you running round this house.'

'I know how you feel, I can't wait to have a child then we will be complete.' I walked round the house, examining every room and piece of furniture. The detail used for the furniture was exquisite. He followed right behind me. When I got to the master bedroom I squealed.

'Oh Richard this is absolutely beautiful, it's just how I imagined our bedroom would be.'

'I designed the house based on your thoughts and the ideas in your scrap book. I hope you don't mind.'

'Mind, I love it.' He smiled and held out his hands. I walked over to him and he held me tight. 'Eva, providing for you is my duty.'

'Thank you,' I said and planted a great big kiss on his nose.

We ended up christening every room in the house that day. As we drove back to our flat in Brixton I looked back at the house and smiled, if this was what marriage was all about then I would swim in everlasting bliss. But boy was I wrong.

VIII

ANTICIPATION

Our first year of marriage was heavenly. I didn't lack or need for anything because we were financially stable in every way. Richard had inherited a small fortune from his grandfather, and therefore showered me with everything imaginable. To top it all, his import and export business was thriving. Richard bought and sold cars for a living which meant that sometimes he was away travelling from one country to the next on business trips. But I didn't mind him being away for a couple of days at a time. To be honest when he got back he made up for his absence in more ways than one. Our love life was extremely active, but unfortunately it wasn't yielding any fruit. By then Richard and I had been trying for a child for over a year but nothing was forthcoming. We had both had physical checkups and our doctor had told us that we were both in good health and should have no trouble conceiving. So we both left our doctor's surgery convinced that it would happen quickly. Our doctor suggested we 'de-stress' and 'have more sex' which we gladly did.

Then six months later as I was making my way to the pub with a few friends from work a sudden dizzy feeling swept over me and unknowingly, I grabbed onto my friend Gertrude. Gertrude was a very close friend of mine from work, we'd been friends going on three years and I would say we knew everything about each other. She was a petite woman, so for me to grab hold of her so suddenly nearly sent her toppling over. She studied me with concern, relieved that she hadn't fallen over.

'Eva, are you OK?' she asked.

'Yes,' I replied stroking my brow. 'I just feel a bit lightheaded.'

'You do look pale,' she said.

'Do l?' I asked with a slight smile. By then I was feeling quite nauseous.

'Yes, you do, let's go back to the office.'

As Gertrude led me into the office building she nodded at the other girls to go on ahead. When we got to our floor, Gertrude took me into the ladies toilets.

'Eva, how long have you been feeling like this?' she asked with a slight grin.

'Why?' I asked, puzzled.

'Just tell me,' she said gently.

'Well… for a couple weeks now I have been feeling unwell, off my food and tired all the time.' I noticed Gertrude nodding in understanding. I looked at her, still puzzled.

'Do you know what's wrong with me?' I asked. Then without any warning my stomach churned and I felt as if it was being ripped out my body in a slow and deliberate way. I ran into one of the cubicles and puked over and over again. When I eventually finished I came out, rinsed out my mouth and splashed water across my face. As I wiped my face down with a napkin, I felt so ashamed.

'Sorry about that Gertrude. I think I might be coming down with something.' I said as I rubbed my tummy. She came over to me and held my hands.

'Eva, when last did you get your period?' she asked with a slight giggle. I suddenly froze, feeling hot and faint. I had been keeping a diary ever since Richard and I had started trying for a baby but I had never been good at keeping track of the mundane workings of my body. I had eventually given up and left nature to take its course. I tried to mentally calculate the dates but the numbers muddled up in my head.

'Oh Gertrude, I can't seem to remember

when, it could be a month or two.' I said feeling dismayed. 'I've been so preoccupied lately on other matters.' She nodded knowingly and smiled.

'I have a feeling you could be pregnant!' she said excitedly.

'You really think so?' I said hopefully.

'I do because you are showing all the signs in the book, there is a pharmacy down the road let's get a pregnancy kit.'

When we got back from the pharmacist, we went into the ladies toilets. I made my way into one of the cubicles and peed on the test stick. I came out of the cubicle and placed the stick by the sink and we both hovered around it and waited. Three minutes later, which seemed like eternity, the strip on the stick turned pink. I froze.

'Oh my God, you're pregnant' Gertrude screamed. I couldn't believe it, I just stared at the stick, after trying for so long it was hard to get my head round the idea that I was going to have a baby.

'Eva, congratulations,' Gertrude said, hugging me.

I snapped back into reality and beamed from ear to ear. I knew Gertrude was genuinely happy for me because she was one of my closest friends who knew how desperately I had been longing for a child.

'Thank you,' I said with tears in my eyes.

'You're welcome, I am happy to have shared this moment with you.'

We left the toilet giggling all the way to our desks. I placed the pregnancy stick in an empty envelope and placed it in my bag. For the rest of the day I was lost in a daydream and time wouldn't move fast enough.

On getting home that night I cooked Richard his favorite meal and waited for him to get back from the office. I felt as if I was floating on air, I was so busy getting everything ready for our moment that I didn't notice that it was midnight. Realisation dawned on me when the grandfather clock his great aunt gave us as a wedding present chimed twelve. It was midnight and Richard wasn't back yet which was strange as he never made a habit of being late. The latest he had ever been was 10.00 pm.

As I walked into my room to get my mobile phone from my handbag, I heard the front door open. I rushed out of the bedroom and relief swept over me as Richard walked in.

'Why are you so late?' I asked him as he made his way to the living room. 'Do you know what time it is?'

He placed his briefcase down on the center table and slowly loosened his tie.

'Eva.' He said dryly. I'm tired and I want to go to bed. Can we talk about it in the morning? I noticed that Richard wasn't looking at me and I could sense an air of annoyance in his tone.

'No,' I said. 'We will discuss it now. I have been worried sick about you. You didn't even bother to call.'

Richard bowed his head a moment and sat down on the sofa.

'Eva, I am terribly sorry for being off with you,' he said, 'but to be honest I am extremely tired, I've had a very busy day at the office.'

I felt awful. 'I'm sorry if I'm being a pain.' My voice sounded a bit weak when I spoke. 'It's just that I had something special planned for us tonight.'

'Oh did you?' he said. 'I am so sorry. So what did you have planned?'

'Well I had a special meal prepared for you.' I said excitedly as I suddenly remembered why I was so agitated in the first place.

Richard stood up and held out his hand and we walked into the dining room together. As Richard sat down, I went into the kitchen to get his meal. Just before I served it I wrote on his plate with a permanent marker pen 'soon to be daddy' and covered the plate with food.

As I entered the dining room, I noticed him shoving his mobile phone in his back pocket. But as I was so eager to tell him the good news I didn't pay mind to it.

I sat opposite him at the dining table and watched Richard eat. It felt like forever before he reached the bottom of the plate. I was already getting quite fidgety but I waited as keenly as a fisherman waiting for a bite. When he eventually got to the bottom of the plate he paused.

'What's this Eva?' he asked as he took a closer look. Suddenly, realisation dawned on him and he stared at me in a daze. He got up and walked round to my side of the table and planted a great big kiss on my lips.

'What was that for?' I asked him cheekily.

'That was for completing our family, I love you.'

'I love you too,' I said as I hugged him deeply. The next day I went to my doctor and he confirmed that I was two months pregnant.

IX

THE TRIP

Two weeks later I went over to my parents' place to pick up my mother. We were going to the airport to meet my dad who had gone to Abuja, the capital of Nigeria, on a business trip for two months. I had agreed to take my mother along for the ride mainly because my plan was to get them together, take them to lunch and then announce my pregnancy. When my dad told us he would be travelling, my mother wasn't too pleased that he would be gone for two months and she made sure she kicked up a big fuss over it too. I could remember the argument like it was yesterday. I had gone to the supermarket to pick up a few things dad would need for his trip, since mother refused to get them for him.

On my return, I interrupted a heated argument between husband and wife.

'You can't just up and go, leaving me here to look after the home for two months!' my mother exclaimed.

'Abigail, you know this trip is important, don't make this more difficult than it is already,' my father said with a sigh.

'No. It's you who's making things difficult; it's you who is so wretchedly obstinate.' My mother practically spat at him. A frightening silence followed. My father frowned slightly but it vanished as quickly as it appeared. He went over to where my mother stood and tried to touch her but she flinched and stepped back. My father smiled.

'I love you Abi, stop pushing me away.' He tried moving towards her again but she pushed him away.

'Samson, you know how I feel about that country, all it's ever brought into our lives is loss and heartache. I can't believe that knowing how I feel you still went behind my back to start up a business and now you want to go there for two months! You must be joking.'

'Abigail,' my dad said sharply his eyes narrowing behind his glasses. 'That country you hate so much is a part of us and a part of what makes us who we are today.' If looks could kill I'm sure my dad would have died that day.

'Maybe it made you into who you are today, but it sure didn't make me into what I've become,' my mother yelled at him. The harsh and contemptuous words went on mercilessly. My father stopped smiling and raised his right hand and for an obscene moment, I thought he was going to strike her. But then his hand fell to his side. I quickly positioned myself in between them.

'You've got to stop this. This constant arguing has to end,' I proclaimed in frustration. My mother turned away.

'Mum, what is your problem? You've always known that dad had intentions of settling in Nigeria when the time was right, so him starting up a business over there is a step towards that goal.' My mother grunted and sat down on the sofa turning her attention back to me.

'Eva, you wouldn't understand,' she said with a sigh.

'What wouldn't I understand?' I asked, coaxing her to continue. Getting my mother to talk about the past was hard work and you had to tread carefully on threads that were on the verge of snapping. But she remained tight-lipped. I moved over and sat beside her. 'I know 'that country' as you love putting it has given you nothing but grief in the past. But don't forget that dad lived through it with you. He went through the same hardships and struggles as you did. It may not have been to the same degree, from what little I can gather, but for you guys to have made it this far on your own is a great achievement. You should be proud of yourselves.' My mother looked at me for the strangest moment then kissed her teeth. I couldn't believe the woman hadn't listened to a word I just said.

'I give up; you can be so selfish sometimes mother,' I said in frustration. My mother ignored me. My father came over, patted me on the back and pulled my mother to her feet.

'Abi, things are not what they used to be. Everything has changed in Nigeria and life is much better. Luckily we have made a very good life for ourselves here, I believe it is time for us to build a life where we came from so that we can leave a legacy for our children and grandchildren.' That seemed to do the trick because she looked over at me and smiled.

'Yes, Samson you are right, it's about time Eva and that husband of hers gave us a grandchild instead of wasting time. I am not getting any younger.' She said all this while looking me up and down without as much as a blink. I felt very uncomfortable. I knew she would be gunning for me next. 'Eva, it's about time your so-called-husband started doing his job, you've been married for 11 months now and you're not even showing any signs of a bump. Are you taking the herbal remedy I brewed up for you?'

My mother had already started to piss me off. She had this habit of never referring to Richard by his given name; she called him every other name under the moon but never Richard. Not wanting another argument I decided to keep tight-lipped. 'Yes mother,' I said sarcastically as I moved into the kitchen. She really knew how to push my buttons in more ways than one.

'That's good if you keep taking it you will be pregnant in no time. Isn't that true Samson?' My father just smiled.

I drove my father to the airport the next day. They both sat at the back. The woman insisted on coming along for the ride, much to my dismay. My mother wasn't someone you wanted to be stuck on a car journey with. But I wasn't too worried because she kept silent all the way to the airport; she just gazed out of the window while holding on tightly to my father's hand. This was a very odd sight for me to witness because this was the most affection I'd ever seen my mother display towards my father. When my father was finally ready to check-in my mother snapped out of her daydream and broke her silence. She hugged my father as if she'd never let go and told him to promise that he would come back to her. My father chuckled.

'Of course I will be coming back Abi, stop being melodramatic. Just take care of my girls for me.' My mother sniffed and hugged him. I went over to my father and hugged him also.

'Take care dad, and make sure you keep in touch.'

My father nodded giving me a big smile then bent over and whispered in my ear.

'Take good care of your mother, she is a big softy at heart.'

'Yeah right,' I said not convinced. My mother has always been the iron lady as far as I was concerned; Margaret Thatcher had nothing on her.

On our journey home my mother was as quiet as a monk. I tried talking to her but with no luck. She was not responsive whatsoever. I didn't blame her though, I knew if Richard went away for two months I wouldn't know where to put

myself. So I left her to it. She was

however; in that mood for most of the

time my father was away.

X

THE RETURN

On arriving at my parents' place, I noticed
that there was a different beat to my
mother's drum. She was very chirpy,
vivacious and full of life. I noticed
everything was squeaky clean. My Mother
had been very busy cleaning, I found her
in the kitchen humming to herself as she
chopped up the salad.

'Hi mum!'

'Hello, Eva, how are you?' she sang at
me.

'Fine,' I said with a frown. Her attitude
lately was unnerving, I'd only seen her
that excited once and that was on my

wedding day.

'So mum are you ready?' I asked.

'No just give me 20 minutes to freshen up.'

'OK,' I yelled back at her as she breezed past me up the stairs. I made my way into the living room and crashed on the sofa, picking up the TV remote at the same time. I'd been itching so badly to tell my mother about the pregnancy but I wanted to wait for my father to get back so I could tell them both at the same time. As I browsed through the TV stations my eyes caught the news headline moving across the screen.

'...*CNN/Africa/Nigerian jet crash leaves 110 dead*'.

My heart skipped a beat. I increased the volume, but how I wished I hadn't because what bellowed out of the TV set that day sent chills up and down my spine. I sat up straight and listened.

'...A Boeing 832 aircraft flight number A1752 has crashed this morning shortly after take-off from Abuja city airport, killing 110 passengers out of the 190 on board. The identities of the passengers have not been released pending notification of relatives. The federal government...'

I couldn't take anymore my heart was beating so fast I thought it would give up.

I went over to the dining table where I had placed my handbag and took out a sheet of paper that contained my father's flight schedule. As I looked at it, fear engulfed me. I ran to the bottom of the stairs and started screaming my mother's name over and over again. She came rushing down the stairs.

'What is it, Eva? She said looking at me in puzzlement. But I just couldn't bring myself to tell her.

'What is it?' she asked impatiently. I pulled her into the living room and told her to sit down, she obeyed without a word. I sat down beside her, tears streaming down my cheeks. I felt choked up as if an apple core had lodged itself inside my throat.

'Eva, what is it?' this time I could sense the fear in her voice. I took a deep breath and let it out.

'Mum, I think dad may have been in a plane crash,' I said trying very hard not to choke. She looked at me and laughed.

'What do you mean, Eva; do you actually think that's funny?'

'Mum, why would I joke about something as serious as that. Look,' I said as I directed her attention to the TV but unfortunately the presenter had moved on to other news.

'What am I supposed to be looking at?' my mother asked impatiently.

'Just wait,' I snapped back at her. Finally it came back on.

'See.' I said and pointed at the screen.

My mum shook her head and smiled knowingly. 'It's not his flight.'

'It is mum, because I've double-checked.'

She got up and went over to the TV, took a closer look, turned round and walked into the kitchen. I followed her calling out her name but she didn't even acknowledge that I was there.

In the kitchen she stopped by the fridge, opened it and brought out the bowl of salad she had been preparing when I walked in earlier. I couldn't believe she was thinking of food at that moment.

'Mum,' I screamed. 'How can you think of food, did you hear what I've just said?'

Ignoring me she walked calmly over to the dining table and started to set the table. By this time I was getting very frustrated and it showed because she finally took notice.

'It is not your father's flight.' This time I shoved the flight schedule into her hands. She looked down at it and blinked twice.

'Well if it's his flight then he is definitely among the survivors,' she said cheerfully.

'I hope so,' I replied feeling a bit ashamed. My mother was being so optimistic and I, on the other hand, was flying off the handle. She came over to me and patted me on both cheeks.

'Well there's nothing for you to worry about because he is among the survivors.'

I looked at her, walked over to the phone and picked it up.

'What are you doing?' she asked.

'I'm calling the airline to find out what

exactly is going on.' But I dialed and redialed but I just couldn't get through. Fifteen minutes later I slammed the phone down in frustration. I started to pace around the living room. My mother walked over to me.

'Eva, what would you like to eat?' she asked. I stopped and looked at her in anger. 'How can you think of food at a time like this, when dad could be dead?' I screamed at her. I saw my mother flinch. I turned round, retrieved the telephone and started to dial.

'What are you doing? My mother asked.

'I'm calling Richard, he needs to be here.'

'Don't you dare call that husband of yours, I don't want him here.' my mother spat out venomously. That did it, something just snapped in me and I just started screaming at her.

'Whether you like it or not mother, Richard is going to be here so deal with it.' My mother stepped back, turned around and went upstairs. I dialed Richard's office and his secretary picked up the phone.

'Hi Linda, could you put me through to my husband please,' I said feeling totally exhausted.

'Hi Eva, sure I'll just connect you,' I heard a click then Richard's rich baritone voice boomed down the line. I burst out crying.

'Darling what's the matter?' He asked concerned. 'Is it the baby?'

'No, Richard, it's not the baby,' I said in

between sobs.

'So what is it then?' he asked.

'Richard, you've got to get down here now, it's... it's…' but I couldn't help myself I started to babble incoherently.

'Calm down, Eva, take a deep breath and tell me what happened,' he asked gently. I did as he said and told him what had happened. When I finished I felt overwhelmed with fear again and I started to cry.

'Eva.'

'Yes, Richard.'

'I'll be right over. How is your mother holding up?'

'Well she's been acting all weird since I told her; she's up in her room right now though.'

'Eva, take it easy with her she must be in shock, give me 45 minutes.'

'OK love, see you soon.' I placed the phone back on its hook. My mother was still upstairs. I made my way to the living room and sat down in front of the TV. I picked up the remote and started searching through the channels to see if I could get the latest on the crash, but nothing new came up just the same headline over and over again. I threw the remote aside in anger.

XI

DREAD

By the time Richard arrived I had finally
got through to the airlines. They
confirmed that my father was on the flight
when the plane left Abuja but they could
not tell me as yet if he was among the
survivors or the dead. This got me so
agitated and frustrated to the point that I
started screaming at the airline
representative over the phone. I just
couldn't understand their inefficiency.
Feeling I wasn't getting anywhere I gave
up and gave her my number to call me
back as soon as she had any news. As I

was replacing the phone the doorbell rang. Richard walked in and my sense of dread lifted. Elated, I launched myself into his arms. He hugged me and guided me to the living room. He always took me out of the dark and into the light.

As we sat down, I filled him in on my phone call with the airline. He reassured me that everything would be alright and we just needed to be thankful at this point in time.

'Where is your mother?' he asked looking round.

'She hasn't come down yet,' I said in disgust.

'Eva, you've got to take it easy on her. She is obviously in shock. Give her time she'll come round soon.' I grunted, folded my arms and stared at the TV. We sat watching the news for what seemed like hours when all of a sudden a fresh bulletin came on.

'…The names of the dead and surviving passengers from Boeing 832 that crashed early this morning as it left Abuja have been confirmed. For information on loved ones please call…'

I jumped up as if I'd been struck by lightning. I rushed to the phone and started dialing, Richard came over and took the phone from me.

'Eva, you go and get your mother, I'll call the airline.' I nodded and dashed up the stairs calling my mother's name. As I ran into her room I found her on her kneels in prayer. I halted by the door and called her name. I felt awful.

'Mum,' I said gently.

'Yes,' she replied without looking up.

'The names have been released, Richard is calling them now to find out if dad is OK.' My mother stood up and walked past me into the corridor and down the stairs in what seemed like a daze. As we approached the living room, Richard set the phone down.

'Is he alright?' I asked excitedly. Richard looked at me and then at my mother.

'I think you need to both sit down.' I heard my mother moan.

'No,' I said sternly. 'Just tell me.'

'Eva...,' his voice trailed off as he

suppressed a cough.

'Richard! Just tell me,' I said again, this time getting a bit irritated.

'Unfortunately, your father's name was among the dead,' he said choking back tears. I stepped back.

'It can't be possible,' I said shaking my head. 'Are you sure?' I asked him.

'Yes, they found some personal belongings on him that I know were only his.'

'It can't be my dad, my dad can't be dead,' I said pleading with him with my eyes.

Suddenly I heard glass shattering. I spun round and my mother was on the ground in a heap, she had fainted and as she fell she had knocked down a vase that was on the table. I ran over to her screaming her name and crying at the same time. Richard picked her up and placed her on the sofa. He bent down and checked her breathing and pulse. I lingered behind scared out of my mind.

'Is she going to be alright?' I asked.

'She is breathing which is a great sign,' he said reassuringly. 'Get me a cold moist towel.'

I ran into the kitchen and came back with one. Richard applied it to her face

'Should I call an ambulance?' I asked.

'Yes, call one.' I rushed over to the phone and dialed 999. By the time the ambulance arrived Richard had managed to revive her. Looking up at me confused my mother asked me why I was crying. This set me off again and I held on to her tightly.

'Dad is dead,' I wailed. She looked at me and her eyes went dark.

'No, he's not; he'll be home soon because he promised me he would.' The doorbell rang at that moment and Richard went to the door. The next thing I knew the paramedics were attending to my mother.

'Mrs. Hamilton, are you alright?' they asked as they fussed around her. She ignored them and looked at me.

'Eva, where is your father?' she asked. I just couldn't take it and I looked over at Richard for help. Richard gave her a hug and held her. But she just totally ignored him and just kept looking at me.

'Eva, where is your father?' she kept on

asking me.

'Mum please!' I said as I knelt down beside her. Richard moved back and I held her hands but just couldn't find the words. She looked over at the paramedics and asked them if they knew where her husband was. When nobody could answer she got up and started searching for my father round the house and calling out his name.

'Mum please stop this,' I pleaded with her but she acted as if I didn't even exist. Feeling very frustrated and angry I went over to her and slapped her back into the real world. She stopped and stood still looking at me with tears in her eyes. Then suddenly she collapsed on the floor and started screaming hysterically. The paramedics rushed to her aid and had to sedate her in order to calm her down. As the paramedics carried my mother away, I cried uncontrollably. If I hadn't had Richard there supporting me I would have ended up beside my mother on the hospital bed.

My mother lost a part of herself that fateful day. She was released from the hospital two weeks later but she had literally gone into a meltdown. Janet, my sister, who was away at university at the time of the tragedy, also took the news very badly. I had to send Richard to drive down to Portsmouth to pick her up. I felt sorry for her, mostly because she was right in the middle of her exams, but also because she was extremely close to our

father.

XII

GOODBYE

Being the first born, it fell on my shoulders to arrange the funeral. My father had always told us as we grew up that in the event of his death, he wanted to be buried in his homeland.

But when I approached my mother about the funeral arrangements she refused point blank. I even asked J's mother to plead with her but my mother stood her ground. This made me lose all hope as she never said no to J's mother. As far as she was concerned '...that country took my husband's soul and I'll be dammed if I'll let it take his body too...' So my father's body was flown back to the UK.

The burial was a melancholic affair. My father, so vibrant, energetic, loving and good-humoured was gone. My mother just stared throughout the ceremony as if she was in a world of her own holding on to J's mother for dear life. When his coffin was finally lowered into the pit below, I squeezed Janet's hand tightly and looked over at my mother. I felt my heart rip out of my chest as I watched her crumble. She was trembling uncontrollably. We threw his favourite carnation into his coffin.

When the ceremony finished, Janet and J's mother, led my mother away. When they had walked a few steps, my sister realised I wasn't following, so she glanced around and looked at me. Our eyes met and she smiled. I knew she understood why I had held back and she continued to lead my mother to the car.

Others who had attended the funeral trickled away from the graveside and out of the cemetery.

Looking at the time, I realised five minutes had passed as I stood at the foot of my late father's grave in the deserted cemetery. The sun was bright and scorching.

Hot, burning tears rolled down my lean cheeks. Apart from myself, there were three other people beside dad's grave. They were the gravediggers erecting a slab on the grave. I watched with a heavy heart as they carried out their assignment, beads of sweat trickling down their backs. Before I left the cemetery that scorching afternoon, I knelt down at the foot of my father's grave and prayed. As I prayed, I wept.

I asked my father to forgive me for not being able to bury him the way he would have wanted. At that moment, I felt a slight breeze on my left cheek. I knew then that he would always be with me. 'Goodbye, daddy,' I whispered into the breeze, 'I'll miss you.'

That night as Richard held me in bed, I felt warm tears slide under my closed lids and onto my hot cheeks. I never wanted to move ever again. My limbs felt heavy, too heavy to stir. I wanted to curl up and sleep as if the day's events had never happened. I wanted to put my hands over my ears and close my eyes so that it would all go away.

Richard heard me whimper and held me closer. He held me in silence until I fell asleep.

Four days after the burial, I went to visit my mother. I had offered for her to stay over at my place for a while but she refused. I didn't push her though, I knew how she could get when she felt pressurised into doing something.

As I drove into the driveway that day I gulped, with the events of the last couple of weeks I hadn't had the chance to tell her that I was pregnant.

Walking into my parents' house it felt

strange, the lack of my father's presence in the house made it feel very cold.

Upon entering the living room, I found my mother sitting in my father's armchair staring into space. She hadn't even noticed that I'd walked into the room. I noticed that she looked very lean, her hair wasn't brushed and she looked like she'd been crying for days. Her eyes were blood red. I knelt down beside her and held her hand. I felt my heart go out to her like it'd never done before. My sister walked into the room and sat on the sofa opposite us. We were like that for a while, and then I felt I had to break the silence.

'Mum, have you been eating?'

'Yes,' she replied, not looking at me.

'I don't think you are because you look so

thin.' She didn't say a word. 'Mum,' I called out once again.

'Eva!' she finally replied impatiently.

'Yeah, mum,' I said, relieved that she had snapped out of her mood.

'Was it my eating habits you wanted to speak to me about?'

'Well, no and yes.'

'So which one is it then?' she asked, not even looking at me once.

'Well, it's about Richard and l?' I noticed as soon as I mentioned Richards's name she shifted slightly in the armchair but she didn't say anything. I stared at her for a long time. I just couldn't believe after all that had happened with the death of my father and how Richard had supported us all emotionally, physically and financially, she still hated him.

'Mum,' I said sadly. 'Why do you hate Richard so much?' She didn't reply. It can get very frustrating, trying to get information out of my mother sometimes. It was like squeezing water out of a stone.

'Mum,' I called her again.

'Just say what you have to say Eva, I'm tired.'

'Well... Richard and I are expecting a baby,' I said with a smile. She looked at me for the first time since I'd been in the room.

'How far gone are you?' she asked not smiling.

'Four months,' I replied.

'It doesn't look as if you've got anything in there,' she said as she looked away again.

'Anyway, how come it has taken you four months to tell me you are pregnant?'

'I'm sorry, I did plan on telling you on the day...' I paused nervously. I didn't want to say anything to upset her, as her moods were unpredictable.

'What day?' She asked.

'The day of dad's intended arrival.' She looked at me long and hard and then frowned.

'You do know it was your fault?

'Pardon?' I asked, looking at her in confusion. My voice had gone up a few octaves.

'If you had kept your stupid my mouth shut and not supported your father when he foolishly decided to go on that godforsaken business trip, then my

Samson would be here with me today,'

she said venomously. By now the initial

shock was over, I couldn't believe my

ears.

'How could you accuse me of such a

horrible thing?' I asked her, nearly busting

into tears. But she just got up and walked

towards the kitchen. I followed behind

calling her name.

Halfway into the kitchen she suddenly

turned round to look at me.

'My eyes have been opened Eva, and I've

seen what you are capable of,' she said

coldly. I looked at her in shock.

'Mum,' I whimpered but she continued

relentlessly.

'After you killed my husband you now

have the audacity to tell me you are pregnant and expect me to be happy?'

I was so shocked by her accusation that I was left speechless. 'I've had enough of you and Richard, so please go back to your husband and leave me alone,' she screamed at me. But I just stood there frozen to the spot. I looked over at Janet who, by now, was crying and just too far gone in her own sorrow to be of any help. 'Mum you don't mean this,' I managed to say. But she just turned round, walked out of the kitchen and up the stairs. As she walked away from me that day I could feel my heart literally rip piece by piece. The hatred I began to feel for my mother from that day, caused me a lot of years of pain, but I finally realised that I was not hurting her, I was hurting myself and I

was in bondage to her because I had a

heart full of hate.

XVIII

LOSS

When Richard got back from work he found me coiled up on the sofa crying my eyes out. He rushed over to me in a panic. 'Eva. What is it? Is it the baby?' he tried to touch my tummy but my coiled up legs were preventing him from reaching his target.

'No,' I said.

'So, what is it?' he asked, sounding relieved. I narrated the day's event to him and when I finished he just sat there, mouth ajar, in disbelief.

'Your mother actually said that to you?' he asked again for the fourth time. I nodded. He begged me to be patient with her because she was in a world of loneliness at the moment. He felt she was lashing out due to the fact she was finding it hard adjusting to life without my father. This calmed me down and I stopped crying. Ten minutes later I fell asleep with my head on Richard's lap.

A while later I woke up feeling a sense of dread. As soon as I opened my eyes I knew something was wrong. I looked around and realised Richard had brought me into the bedroom.

As I tried to get up I noticed my thighs where a bit sticky. Getting up I looked down at the bed and froze. I realised that I had bled quite badly on the sheets. I let out a scream and Richard came rushing into the room.

'Eva, what is it?' he asked breathlessly.

I couldn't speak so I just pointed at the

bed and started to whimper. He

immediately dialed the ambulance service.

When he had called, he rushed over to me

and tried to sit me down on the bed but I

wouldn't budge. Then suddenly I felt an

excruciating bout of pain. The pain was

unbearable. Richard carried me to the

bathroom and took of my clothes while

trying to calm me down at the same time.

He placed me in the shower and ran the

water. I just stood there crying and

wailing, I could see the fear in Richards's

eyes. A new bout of pain overwhelmed

me so much that I crouched down and by

the time I saw the fetus on the floor in the

shower I fainted.

When I came to, I realised I was on a
hospital bed. I looked round my
surroundings in a daze. I could hear
somebody crying in the room. I tried to
focus on where the sound was coming
from, but I couldn't make out who or what
was there. I still felt a bit woozy.

I whispered Richards's name. The crying
stopped and I heard him answer me.
'Yes,' he said, approaching the bed. He
held my right hand and I gazed up at him.
He looked as if he'd aged overnight.
He then burst out crying like a baby. I
knew what had happened. He didn't need
to tell me, I could read it in his eyes.
Gently removing my hand from his, I

rolled up into a ball and wished the
ground would swallow me whole.

Seven minutes later, the doctor came
round and explained to me that I'd had an
incomplete miscarriage and some
pregnancy tissue still remained inside the
uterus. He said that I would need to have a
dilatation and curettage operation due to
the risk of an infection developing.

As he went even further into his
explanation I zoned out. I couldn't hear a
word he was saying but I could see his
mouth move. I glanced over at Richard.
As he listened to the doctor, he looked
downcast. The doctor reassured us that the
miscarriage hadn't caused any side effects
and we should be able to have another
child.

I was released from the hospital later that night. The drive home was a pitiful one. Neither Richard nor I said a word to each other. I did catch him though, through the course of the drive home, stealing a glance at me. But I acted as if I didn't acknowledge him. I was lost in a world of my own.

I felt then that whatever heartache life brought my way after that day nothing would be as bad as the gift I'd lost. Unfortunately, I didn't realise then that what life had in store for me in the upcoming years was beyond my wildest dreams.

XIV

Friendship

During the time of the Roman Empire, Marcus Tullius Cicero, a great Roman philosopher had his own beliefs on friendship. Cicero believed that in order to have a true friendship with someone there must be honesty and truth. If there isn't, then this isn't a true friendship. In that case, friends must be 100 per cent honest with each other and put 100 per cent of their trust in the other person. Finally, the last thing that Cicero believed was that the reason a friendship comes to an end is because one person in that friendship has become bad. His philosophy was one that I had always kept close to my heart. His philosophy portrayed the friendship that I thought I had with J. Our friendship was supposed to last forever; it was based on trust, honesty and love. But as I look back I realise that life has a way of changing things, transforming people, places and things from the way they were in the beginning.

Joshua Theodore Adams or J, as I liked to call him, had been my best friend since preschool. We were inseparable. My mother and his were best friends. I only ever saw my mother giggle like a school girl when Aunty Georgina was around. My father always ended up excusing them and leaving them to it anytime she came round. I could tell my father always felt like a third wheel when they were all together. Their encounters always left me baffled as the change in my mother was unbelievable. So, one day I decided to ask my father why the two women were so close. My father smiled at me that day, folded the newspaper he was reading in two and patted the seat beside him. I sat down next to him and looked at him eagerly. My father cleared his throat and began.

'You remember I told you how your mother and I came to live in the UK?' 'Yes,' I answered him nodding. 'Due to the Biafran war.' My father smiled and continued.

'Well, Aunty Georgina also fled the war.'

'What!' I said looking at him surprised. 'I didn't realise that. So, did they also meet each other in the UK like you and mum did?'

'No,' my father replied. 'Their story was before my time.'

'Oh.' I said looking shocked but urging him to tell me more.

'Well, your mother and Aunty Georgina met each other at a refugee camp during the war. They were drawn together like two kindred spirits.

I held my breath, I was getting excited as this was more information in one breath than I knew about my mother.

'Wow, a refugee camp?' I asked my dad excitedly. He nodded and continued.

As you know by now your mother came from a very poor family. Your grandparents planted crops and reared cattle. Your grandmother died giving birth to your mother leaving your grandfather to raise her on his own. When the burden became too much he was forced to remarry his late younger brother's wife and take in their two children.

'What!' I exclaimed looking baffled. 'His late brother's wife?' I asked looking totally bewildered.

'Yes.' My father answered. This is called marriage by inheritance or levirate - whereby a widow may become the wife of her brother-in-law. I gave my dad a mystified look. He could tell I was finding it very hard to swallow the whole marrying one's own late brother's wife idea.

He explained further that marriage was not all about starting a new family only. The noble institution is not an intercourse only opportunity offering union, but caring for someone that is less fortunate so that she would have relief from her misfortune and love that she lost. I nodded at my father in understanding and urged him to continue his story. My father cleared his throat again, then continued:

'Cattle, crops and goods were destroyed when the bombs fell. About 70% of people in her village were killed. The dead included your grandfather, his wife and her two children. Your mother was among the few that fled the village. She packed

up all her belongings into a basket and

placed it on her head and joined the other

survivors as they left the village for the

nearest refugee camp. Your mother was

just 16 when she left her village that day.'

XV

THE CAMP

'It took them three days, along narrow
bush paths, through the rain forest. The
paths were a few feet from the River
Niger which was their only source of
drinking water. They meet other survivors
that day on the path who were also
making their way to the camp. Your
mother noticed that by the time they
reached their destination, not all who
started the journey together made it. Some
had died on their way due to their injuries,
others were killed and some just gave up.
The ones who did make it were tired and
wary, hungry and emaciated from the 70

mile trek.

'Your mother had been at the camp for three days before she noticed a heavily pregnant girl who, looked about her age, sitting on a large rock at the far end of the camp. Your mother felt pity for her so she walked over to say hello.

'As she approached the girl, your mother asked if she was alright. She didn't reply at first she just continued scanning the camp with her eyes. When her attention diverted back to your mother, she smiled wryly.

'"Yes, I'm fine," she said, and continued looking around as if she was hoping to see someone she knew.

'Your mother asked the girl if she would like a drink of water and she noticed that she shifted uncomfortably on the rock as she held on tightly to her tummy. The girl looked down at the water bottle in your mother's hand and smiled at your mother. This time the smile reached her eyes. The girl nodded and your mother passed over the water bottle. As she drank thirstily, your mother observed the girl. She noticed that she came from a wealthy family as she was wearing expensive attire. She also noticed that she was wearing a wedding ring. As the girl continued to swallow the water hungrily, your mother had to caution her on the amount she was drinking as water was like gold dust. The girl passed over the water bottle and thanked your mother.'

'Your mother asked her if she was there with anybody but the girl looked away and began to cry. Your mother closed the gap between them and, sitting on the rock beside her, reached over and held her until her cries finally subsided.

'The girl looked at your mother sadly and stared into the distance. She sighed deeply and began her story.'

XVI

GEORGINA

'My husband had paid a man to get us abroad. He had arranged for us to meet the man at the city of Port Harcourt. We drove out of our town with all the belongings we held dear. On reaching the motorway my husband started to drive extremely fast looking straight ahead and not even taking a sideward glance towards hitchhikers along the road. The motorway, as you know, before the war was a dangerous place to stop for anyone as you were highly likely to be robbed by arm robbers or even killed by them so my husband wasn't taking any chances.

'We continued on the motorway and my husband noticed through the rearview mirror, flashing headlights behind us trying to get us to pull over. My husband reached over to me and squeezed my hand.

'"Hold on dear," he said. "I think we've got trouble."

'Holding on to the wheel he floored it. I turned round to look behind us and I saw a 4x4 Jeep approaching very fast. I held on to my bump tightly and looked over at husband. I noticed he was sweating profusely. He was concentrating so hard in trying to get as far away from the Jeep behind us that he didn't notice the spikes on the road until it was too late.

'He drove over them and we heard a loud bang. I screamed and my husband groaned loudly. Our Jeep started to sway dangerously left and right. I just screamed and screamed as my husband tried to steady the Jeep. He eventually did get the Jeep under control but he didn't stop, he just kept driving until the headlights became like stars in the distance.

'Eventually, he had to park on the side of the road as the Jeep started to make an unbearable noise due to the rims scrapping on the road. We didn't know where we were as it was too dark to see. There were bushes on either side of the road.

'My husband told me to wait as he got out of the car to inspect the damage to the wheels. Popping my head out of the window I asked him if everything was OK. He walked over to my side of the car and when he approached me he reached out and touched my face.

'"The wheels are totally damaged, I don't know how we made it this far." he said as he looked in the direction we were coming from.

'"Oh my God!" I exclaimed. "What are we going to do now?"

'He scratched his head repeatedly as he always did when he was in deep thought.

'"I don't know," he said, looking around us. "It looks like we will have to walk."

'"Walk!" I exclaimed, looking down at my bump. He looked at me worriedly.

'"Darling it is too dangerous for us to wait here, whoever is in those Jeeps may still be tailing us. We need to get going now."

'He glanced nervously once more towards the direction in which we came and walked to the back of the car.

'"Come on Georgina get out of the car and let's go."

'I hurriedly got out of the car as my husband was shoving the things he felt were most valuable to us into a duffle bag. I waited beside him as he packed. I kept looking up the road anxiously. Then I saw it - a glimpse of headlights in the distance. I froze and reached out for my husband, squeezing tightly on his arms. He looked over his shoulder and immediately stopped packing, closed the duffle bag and shoved it into my hands.

"'What are you doing?" I asked looking at the bag.

"'We don't have any more time Georgina, they are upon us. Please I want you to run, into the bushes and hide."

'I hesitated, looking at him in confusion.

"'What about you?" I asked.

'Giving me a smile he held my head in his. "I would rather die than let them get their hands on you two. Please go and hide while I draw them away."

'As he said that, he pressed an envelope into the palms of my hands. I looked down at the envelope.

"'What is this?" I asked.

'"The envelope contains some money and the details of my contact in Port Harcourt. When you find him he will arrange for you to be smuggled into a boat that will take you to the UK."

'"Why are you giving it to me?" I asked. "I thought we were going together?"

'"Don't worry Georgina," he said, hurriedly ushering me into the bushes.

'"Go further into the bushes and crouch down and wait until they go. If I don't come back please make your way to the Refugee camp I will catch up with you as soon as I can."

'My husband hugged me tightly then shoved me into the bush.

'"Run," he shouted. I gave him one last look of despair and hurriedly entered the bushes. I started to run, dragging the duffle bag behind me. I glimpsed over my shoulder and saw my husband sprinting away in the distance. I noticed that instead of the one Jeep we had seen, there were now two. One slowed down and parked alongside our Jeep while the other sped down the road trailing my husband.

'I heard shouts of "hey stop there." But I didn't stop I just kept running, struggling all the while with the duffle bag. Reaching a distance, I stopped as I could not run anymore. I collapsed onto the ground unable to move any further. I wanted my husband back so desperately. I looked back towards the way I came, stood up and started running.

'As I approached the edge of the bush I noticed two men looting our Jeep. I got on all fours and hid in the bushes watching them. When they finished they got into their Jeep and flashed their headlights. I noticed they were signaling to the other Jeep which was parked not too far down the road. I couldn't see their faces I could only make out their silhouette by the light of the moon.

'The other Jeep turned round and headed towards the one parked near to ours. When they approached the two Jeeps signalled to each other by flashing their headlights and drove off.

'I stayed put for a while and when it looked like they were definitely gone for sure, I crept out of my hiding place. Walking back to our Jeep I looked inside and noticed they had salvaged everything. I moved to the front of the car looking towards the direction in which my husband had ran hoping to God I could catch a glimpse of him in the distance. Then I noticed something on the ground not too far off from where the other Jeep had parked. My heart skipped a beat and I started to run towards the figure on the ground.

'As I got closer my heart began to sink further into my chest. I realised that it was my husband before I even reached the body. I let out a wail that was sure to be heard from miles away. I ran to my husband's body and fell on top of him screaming his name over and over again. But I got no answer. I cried and cried in frustration and anger beating his chest repeatedly, feeling angry that he left me all on my own.

'As I sat there next to his dead body I heard a rustling in the bushes. I froze and looked to my left and noticed that the bushes were moving. I didn't know who or what was coming my way but I closed my eyes and braced myself to be united with my husband. I suddenly heard whispering and I opened my eyes. Coming out of the bush were two women and a man. I looked at them in bewilderment.

'One of the women approached me and helped me to get up. They informed me that they had seen everything as they themselves were walking alongside the motorway when we first approached hoping they could hitch a ride. They started making their way to our Jeep when they realised there was trouble by the way the two Jeeps were speeding towards us. So they decided to take cover in the bushes and wait out whatever was about to happen.

'They told me one of the guys in the Jeep had leaned out the window and shot my husband when he refused to slow down.

They noticed another man getting out of the car and searching my dead husband's body but could not find anything. I looked down at my husband and started crying again. The other woman came over and guided me away from the body.

'"Don't worry my dear it will be alright," she said smiling. "Our husband is leading us to the refugee camp, come with us. You will be safer at the camp than out here on your own."

'I knew she was right. I looked over at my husband's body one final time before I allowed myself to be guided along.

'We eventually arrived at the camp two days later and exhausted. Please do not ask me how we got here as I was in a trance like state throughout the journey.'

'Your mother looked at the girl in total disbelief. She just couldn't imagine how anyone could go through such an ordeal in her condition could still be standing.

"Where are the man and his wives now?" your mother asked.

"They went to see if they could get something to eat and told me to wait here." Your mother smiled at her and the girl smiled back.

"What's your name?" The girl asked your mother.

"Abigail Nkechi Okoye."

"Nice to meet you," she said, "my name is Mrs Georgina Ifeoma Adams."

'She gave your mother a hug and they sat

on that rock looking into the distance

together like two kindred spirits. From

that day on your mother and Georgina

were inseparable.'

XVII

THE JOURNEY

'During the next few days, both your mother and Georgina were on a mission to locate the contact Georgina's husband had paid to smuggle them out of the country. By now Georgina had already convinced your mother to accompany her on the journey. There was an extra space since her husband would no longer be going along with her. Your mother was reluctant at first but after Georgina pleaded with her, she felt she couldn't leave her friend to take this unknown path alone so she decided to go with her.

'It didn't take them that long to locate the contact as whispers had already been circulating the camp about a man who could smuggle you out of the country in a cargo boat if you had the money to pay for your passage. Your mother and Georgina did not indicate to anyone that they already had a pass onto the cargo boat. They just sat and listened as people talked. If they had indicated in any way that they had this great opportunity at their fingertips, they may not have survived the night as people would have killed to have one of those passes.

'As they sat back and listened they were able to get information about the meeting point, not too far from the camp, where the contact would be picking up the lucky

few up. Neither your mother nor Georgina

were actually sure if this was true or not as

most of this information came via

whispers in the dark. They both felt it was

a risk worth taking. They were not sure of

the time when the contact would come

but, from what they could gather, he was

due to arrive at the spot in two days' time.

'Two days later, as soon as the sun went

down, your mother and Georgina snuck

out of the camp and made their way to the

meeting place. It took them 30 minutes to

walk to the location. Georgina found it a

struggle but your mother helped and

edged her on every step of the way, and

this gave her strength.

'It was very dark by the time they got to the location. They didn't stand out in the open as these where harsh times. They went into the bushes not too far from the spot and crouched down and waited. The wait felt like forever but after three hours had passed they heard the sound of a vehicle approaching. As they peeped out of their hiding place, they noticed a cargo truck parked not too far from where they were hiding. It had a shipping crate on the back of it but still they waited until they were sure that this was their contact.

'A man got out of the truck and walked to the back of the truck. He opened it and looked inside, turned around and looked towards the bushes. He then reached into his back pocket and brought out a flashlight. He raised the light towards the bushes and flashed it twice at different points. Suddenly, they saw four people; three men and one woman, come out from different corners of the bushes and walk towards the man. Your mother and Georgina hesitated for a while until they noticed that these individuals were giving the man something before they revealed themselves, reassuring them that this was their contact. As they emerged from the bushes and moved towards the man, he looked over at them. As they approached they noticed that the four people had climbed into the back of the cargo truck. When they got to the truck he spread out the palm of his hand and Georgina reached into her bra and brought out the envelope her husband had given her and placed it in his palm. The man looked through the contents of the envelope hungrily. When he finished, he told them to get in. The inside of the truck was dark but enough light shone into the truck from the moon for them to notice that, apart from the four people they saw get into the truck, five others where crouching down in a corner. They all looked at each other solemnly. Suddenly the door to the back of the truck was pulled shut and it became pitch black. Your mother pulled Georgina to the corner of the truck and they huddled there together as the truck began to move.

'They travelled for a long way before finally reaching their destination. As the truck stopped your mother and Georgina held on to each other tightly. The truck was at a standstill for what felt like forever until, eventually, they felt themselves being lifted in the air. They travelled like that in the air until they were finally put down. They were all like this for what seem like an hour when the doors of the crate were suddenly pulled opened and the light from the moon shone through.

'Your mother noticed that there were now two men instead of the one they had seen earlier. The taller one of the two nodded at the other who reached into the large bag he was holding and rolled several large bottles of water into the crate as well throwing in some loaves of bread. As they rushed to retrieve the items the man told them not to finish the supplies all at once. He also informed them that they were now on a cargo ship and that they would be sailing to Europe. From this point onwards nobody would approach their crate until they reached their destination. Before anyone could object to what he had just said the crate was closed.

'Your mother and Georgina's journey was one of the most horrendous voyages they had ever taken. Georgina became very ill during the journey as a result of her pregnancy. Their journey was not made all at once. They ended up in North Africa for a period of time, and then they moved on.

'At times they were squeezed into exceptionally small spaces in trucks or onto unseaworthy boats in order for the smugglers to maximise their "cargo". Your Aunty Georgina gave birth to Joshua on the way but this didn't stop them; they kept on striving. They knew as long as they had each other they could survive anything. Their struggles didn't end there when they got into the UK they went through three months of sleeping rough in fear of been deported by the authorities. They had to beg for food and money in order to survive. It got to a point that Joshua became quite ill and he cried constantly. They didn't know what to do as they were too scared to approach any hospital. They decided to approach an old woman that lived not too far from their frequented spot. This particular old woman had taken a shine to them. She made it a habit in handing them food and clothes especially for Joshua. She had offered to take them to a local shelter but they declined for fear they might be deported.'

'Luckily, as they approached the woman's house they saw her coming out. Your mother rushed to her and asked for her help. The woman beckoned to Georgina to come over. When she did the woman looked at Joshua and gasped. She informed them that it looked like Joshua had the measles and that he should be taken to the hospital immediately. Your mother and Georgina hesitated but the old woman reassured them that everything would be OK and that she would accompany them.

'When they reached the hospital, Joshua was examined by a doctor but he didn't say a word to the two women and instead beckoned for the old woman to come over. He had a few words with her then walked off giving them one final look. They asked the woman what he had said and she informed them that the doctor was very worried that Joshua was extremely ill. He would need to be kept in hospital overnight to monitor him. Georgina was

so scared that that all she did was nod in

agreement and collapse on a seat in tears.

'While they waited, the old woman asked

your mother to get something for them to

eat from the vending machine while

Georgina stayed by Joshua's bedside. On

her way back your mother noticed two

policemen and talking to the old woman

and the doctor. She froze on the spot. Just

then she noticed another policeman

coming out of the room, this time holding

on to Georgina and leading her away. As

soon as your mother saw this she

screamed Georgina's name. This captured

everyone's attention and they all looked in

her direction. As soon as the doctor saw

your mother, he pointed towards her. So, without thinking, your mother just high-tailed it out of there.

'The two policemen gave chase but she just kept running. She made it out of the hospital and as far away as possible. When she finally stopped to catch her breath she realised what she had done. She had left her best friend behind. Your mother, at this point, was so scared she didn't know what to do.

'She made her way back to the hospital and hid not too far away from the entrance. She eventually saw the policemen getting into their van with poor Georgina in the back. As they drove away that day, your mother felt as if her heart had been ripped out.

'She ended up wandering the streets for three months before she was approached by an elderly lady who felt pity for her and took her in.

'Both Georgina and your mother lead a very different life for a short time from that point onwards but they both survived. Their paths crossed again eventually and they have stuck together ever since. The rest is now history.'

I looked at my father in utter amazement, not wanting him to stop.

'Wow!' I said. 'They both went through

all that?'

My father nodded. *'Now I understand why their friendship is so strong,'* I said to myself.

My father smiled and stroked my hair. I saw a hint of something in his eyes that day that I couldn't place. His eyes darkened for a few seconds but he brightened up almost immediately as my mother walked into the living room. They exchanged a look and a message passed between them, all I knew was that my father understood whatever my mother told him with her eyes and responded by picking up his paper and dismissing me cheerfully.

As I walked out of the living room that

day I looked back at my mother. I knew she had been listening to our conversation. Janet had caught her a few times listening in on my conversations with my father. Back then I felt that there was some secret she didn't want my father to tell me and that was why she always made a habit of interrupting our conversations.

XVIII

BETRAYAL

A year after my father's death and the loss of my pregnancy. I wanted us to have another baby but the response I was getting from Richard wasn't the one I hoped for. I'd been noticing a change in him since he got back from the States. He had had to spend eight months over there in order to expand his business. As Richard was planning to spend so long there, I had suggested he stayed with J who now resided there permanently. J had moved to the States to be closer to his sister, as she had lost the use of her legs, and he wanted to be more of a support to her and her family. I felt it would be cheaper than staying in a hotel. J wasn't too happy about this arrangement at first but l talked him round.

During the time Richard was away I was extremely lonely. I missed him so much it felt like a part of me was missing. At the beginning we talked every day but the calls became less frequent. When I complained about not been able to get hold of him as often as I would like, he laughed it off and told me that trying to get his business up and running over in the States was not as easy as he had thought. He said that I shouldn't worry and he'd be home soon. Counting the days to his return made the days bearable for me.

However, when Richard did eventually return back to the UK I noticed a change in him. He wasn't as affectionate as he used to be. Gone were the days he would walk by and smack my buttocks, or grope my breast or twist my nipples whenever he felt like it. All he did now was either work on his laptop till late whenever he was at home or go into the office. He was always coming up with a reason why we couldn't go to dinner or the movies or the theatre or even spend time together. He just seemed preoccupied. Even during our meal times he was as quiet as a mouse. He became very distracted and snappy at every little thing I said or did. I let it ride for a while as I presumed his bad behaviour was due to his new business in the States not generating as much revenue as he had hoped.

He started to come back home late from work some days even pushing it to 2.00 am. I started to feel even lonelier than when he was away. Because, even though I now had him in my grasp, he was slipping away with each waking moment. I eventually got to a point where I stopped getting supper ready for him, as he came in too late to eat the meal. He always ended up falling asleep on the sofa. The sofa by now had become his best friend and I ended up sleeping alone most nights. The days he did come to bed, it felt like I had a stranger beside me for the night. Lying with our backs to each other, the short distance between us felt like a cold gulf that we couldn't cross, even if we wanted to.

In a way, the mornings were worse. We either sat together in silence, Richard hidden behind a newspaper or, as was more common now, he got up early and was gone even before I could wake up and start to fix his breakfast.

I cried myself to sleep in silence most nights. My hot, salty tears were the only give-away. Why wouldn't he just stroke my shoulder gently with one finger and pull me over to him like he used to? One night, I suddenly remembered the Victoria's Secret lace sleepwear that Richard had bought me a long time ago. He had bought me quite a few beautiful things since then, of course, but that one was the first. That was the special one, so I slipped it on and took a look at myself in the mirror. Not bad. I was still admiring the gorgeous lace outline, when I heard the front door bang loudly. Today, Richard was home earlier than I expected. I stood, frozen to the spot. Should I change? I heard him switch on the TV and then start to head upstairs. As the door handle turned, I stared at the opening door in the full length mirror in front of me. I felt like a deer caught in the headlights, but a large part of me was thrilled. Richard looked as handsome as ever. The first thing he saw was my back, and then our eyes met in the mirror. It should have been an emotionally charged and romantic moment, but in his eyes I only saw a steely gaze.

It was almost as if he had not seen me at all. He threw his jacket onto the bed and went through to the bathroom. I heard him turn the shower on.

Suddenly, a chill ran down my spine. Was this how it was going to be from now on? How could he ignore me like this?

I put on a dressing gown.

When he came out of the shower, I was waiting for him. He came into the bedroom with a white towel wrapped around his middle, rubbing his hair with a smaller towel. Beads of water still glistened on his chest and a little steam rose gently from his shoulders.

'Richard.'

'What is it, babe?' he said with a surprised smile.

'I want to talk to you.'

He sat down on the bed and stared at me. The smile on his face was almost like the way he used to smile at me when we first met. Almost.

'What's happened?' I demanded.

'What do you mean, what's happened?' he replied.

'I mean, what's happened to us? We don't talk anymore. We haven't made love for as long as I can remember.'

Richard stopped rubbing his hair. 'Eva,' he mocked, 'yes we have.'

'No, Richard, we haven't,' I said. 'I thought we were supposed to be trying for another baby.' I was on the verge of tears but I held them back.

'I don't think you love me anymore,' I said.

'Babes!' he said. 'Of course I do!'

He came over to me and gave me the most awkward hug ever.

Kneeling by my side, he stroked my hair.

'Look,' he said earnestly, staring into my eyes. 'I've been really busy trying to get this business sorted out. It's tiring you know?'

It was a perfect moment. Richard knelt at my feet in a bath towel, while I sat in my bathrobe in my sexiest sleepwear. I felt closer to him than I had for a very long time.

He looked up at me. 'OK?' he said.

'Yes, my darling,' I replied.

Then he got up and went back into the bathroom. When he came back out he was dressed and dry. I had turned down the lighting down and was lying on the bed waiting seductively for his return, but just then his phone bleeped.

He looked at me as if he was really caught short. 'I'll just see what that is, OK?'

'Oh, honey, can't you just leave it until the morning?' I pleaded, not wanting to ruin the moment.

'I'll just check it?' he said and took the phone downstairs.

I waited an hour, and then I had had enough. Tiptoeing downstairs, I saw that Richard had fallen asleep on the sofa.

I wanted to shake him! I wanted to shout at him and ask why he was treating me like this? But instead, I turned and went back up to my bedroom and spent nearly the whole night with hot tears running down my cheeks.

The next morning, he was gone. He had left early as usual. There was a note on the kitchen counter. It read: *'Didn't want to wake you, I'll be late home, don't wait up.'*

I was getting close to the last straw. How could he treat me like this? I was determined to get to the bottom of it. That night, I waited up for him. No matter how long it took, I was determined to have it out with him and finally find out what was going on. While I was sitting lost in my thoughts, the darkness slowly gathering in around me, I heard his car pull up outside.

It was nearly 2 o'clock in the morning, so it could only be him.

I went to the curtain and pulled it aside to peep out into the street.

I could see Richard's face lit up by the street lamp. Just as he was about to open the door, his phone lit up. He stared at the phone for a second and then pressed the accept button. Even from here I could see how angry Richard was as he took the call. He was almost shouting down the line. As the call ended, I could feel his frustration, as he threw the phone forcefully onto the back seat. He sat back for a moment, staring into the night, his face shrouded with gloom. I watched, fascinated. I was sure that he could not see me. Suddenly, I jumped. Richard had slumped forward onto the dashboard, with his arms resting on the steering wheel. What was happening? I ran to the door, but when I opened it, he was standing there. There was such a shocking look on his face.

'Richard,' I began.

He tried to push past me and get into the house.

'Richard,' I said again, this time much more forcefully. 'Where the hell have you been?'

'Eva,' his voice faltered as if he was trying to think of something to say. Obviously he was not expecting me to be waiting for him.

'No, Richard, you tell me where you have been until 2.00 am.' I said.

'Eva, please, just let me in, I'm really tired.'

'No Richard, first you tell me what you've been up to.' I said. 'I called your office,' I lied.

His gaze shifted and he looked right at me as if he was seeing me for the first time.

'You what? Have you been spying on me?' he yelled.

'Well,' I said, thinking fast, 'is there something worth spying on? You're having an affair aren't you?'

'What?!' he yelled. 'Just let me in, Eva, this is ridiculous.'

But I would not open up the door for him. I wanted answers. I wanted to know where he had been.

'Who was that on the phone just now?'

He stared at me. It was beginning to rain and he was starting to get wet standing there, but I was not going to let him come in until I knew what was going on.

'I'm not having this,' he said. Instead of pushing his way in, he stormed off, back to the car.

I was angry with him, but I wanted to face him and thrash it out. The last thing I wanted was for him to run off.

'Wait!' I yelled at the top of my lungs. 'You come back here!'

I chased him to the car, but he was already in the driver's seat. Blindly, I followed and banged my fists on the windscreen scattering drops of rain in all directions. But it was no use. I shouted and screamed, but I could see his jaw set firm in the driver's seat as he glared into my face. He backed away from me and with a screeching handbrake turn, drove off down the road. I was left screaming his name in the rain. When a couple of lights went on the neighbours' houses, I suddenly realised where I was. Self-consciously I trudged back to the house which had once been my dream home.

The next day I waited on tenterhooks to see what he would say when he walked through the door. Was I imagining things? Maybe he was just trying to sort out the business. But he would not have put me through all these weeks of coldness if that was the case, surely?

I tried calling him but his phone went to voicemail after a few rings. So I played the waiting game. Trying to keep myself busy all day until the time when he would be coming home.

It turned out that I was in the garden when he did return. I had gone out for a second into the sunshine and when I came inside, his jacket was lying on the couch.

'Richard?' I called, but there was no reply. Tiptoeing to the top of the stairs, I realised that he must have jumped straight into the shower when he came home. This was my chance to prove to myself once and for all that everything was normal.

So I fumbled through his pockets, looking for the phone. My fingers were shaking and jittery as I finally found it and started to work through to the call log. I wanted to see what was making him act so strangely. With one ear constantly on the noise of the shower, I worked through the call log and then to the messages. There was nothing. It was all full of my messages. All the calls were from me and all the calls he made were made to my phone. I could not understand it. I was still standing there staring at it when I suddenly realised that the shower had stopped. How long had it been? Fear crawled around my stomach and I quickly dropped the phone back into his jacket pocket as if it was suddenly hot.

I crept downstairs, but I knew. And the knowledge was beginning to haunt me: Richard had another phone. All the calls he was taking were on that phone. I wanted to curl up into a ball and die. Why had this man, who was my life partner, suddenly turned his back on me? I racked my brain trying to think about what I'd done. But came up with a blank.

Sitting in the lounge, I waited for him to come downstairs. The expectation of what was to come turned my body to a jelly. I could feel my arms shaking with nervousness.

But when he came down, he was fully dressed. He glanced in my direction, but did not say anything to me, instead, he made his way over to the door.

'Richard?'

'I have to go to a business meeting,' he grunted without looking at me. And then he opened the door and left.

This time I was determined to find out

where he was going. I waited until I heard his car drive away and then rushed out of the house, grabbing my car keys. I had never followed anyone before, but I knew that I had to stay back and not be seen. Luckily, it was so dark that he would not be able to recognise my car too easily. After following him for around 20 minutes, I realised that he was not heading to his office. He was going into the center of town. Puzzled, I saw him park and then go into one of the really fancy hotels, the Grand Hotel, which was supposed to be a swanky five star location.

After a few moments, I followed him in. Luckily, I was wearing a figure-hugging purple, low cut dress as I was planning to ask Richard to go out to dinner so that we could talk things over. So, I did not feel out of place at all.

Inside, the carpet was deep, the lighting was low and the decorations were lavish. It was a luxurious place. I saw no sign of Richard so I went over to the bar and ordered a cocktail. It was slightly daunting sitting there on my own and I avoided making eye contact with at least three different men who were sitting at the bar. I made my way over into the hotel lounge, trying to figure out what to do next. I thought about it. If Richard walked in, I could pretend that I was waiting for a girlfriend.

Suddenly, the lift at the far end of the lobby 'pinged' and the doors opened. A few people got out and, in amongst them,

I thought I caught a glimpse of Richard's head. It was not easy to see in the crowd, but I was becoming more and more sure that one of the men was Richard. When two of the men broke away from the small crowd coming out of the lift, I was positive. One of them was definitely Richard, dressed the in the dark grey suit I had seen him in when he had left the house. The other man was just as tall as Richard and although I did not see his face, he moved easily and gracefully. They were standing discussing something. So it was a business meeting. They made their way towards the bar and I could still see them from where I was sitting as they ordered drinks.

Richard's face looked even more

handsome in the subtle lighting of the bar. His business partner had his back to me, but from the way they were talking, it seemed as if they were discussing something quite important. Should I go and join them? Why not? It was such a relief to see that Richard had been telling the truth that I could actually feel the tension leaving my body.

I got up happily and started walking towards them, watching them talk. Suddenly, I stopped in my tracks. The guy with his back to me took hold of Richard's chin with his hand and leant forwards and kissed him on the lips. Richard looked a little stunned, but after a second, he looked at the guy's lips, and I saw Richard's hand wander to his bottom, under his jacket and then he responded passionately. They kissed like old lovers. Richard came up for air and smiled broadly at the other guy. I felt like I had been hit with something. I just couldn't believe it. My head felt tight as if I was going to faint. I heard my voice say, 'Richard,' faintly.

He looked up and, seeing me, his smile froze onto his face. He looked trapped, his eyes widening with shock.

The other guy, seemed to be lost in the mood, but seeing Richard's expression, turned around to face me and I finally saw who it was. It was... even now, I shudder as I think of it. I stood looking at J for what seemed like forever.

How could I have been so blind? I ran,

unseeing from the hotel, in a rage and at a loss. As I ran out of the hotel lobby I heard Richard screaming my name. But I didn't look back. Tears flooded down my face but I did not notice them. All I could think of was to get away. As far away as possible.

Suddenly, I noticed myself sitting in my car, driving home. He had betrayed me to the core of my being. Hardly noticing where I was going, my instinct led me to the one place where I had known some happiness, even if it was a long time ago. Coming out of my daze, I realised that I had driven home, to my mother's house. It was a wrench to park the car and walk up to the front door. Knowing my mother, I knew that she would have something to say about how she always knew Richard was a bad one, but I could not go home. How could I?

I went inside and called out, 'Mum?' softly. I did not want to shock her by turning up unexpectedly, but there was no reply.

'Mum?' I repeated. Everything was still in confusion. My whole body felt numb and my head throbbed from the crying.

Eventually, I went upstairs. My mother was probably in her room. I pushed the door open softly and what I saw gave me another shock.

My mother was sitting on the floor surrounded by old letters and envelopes. She looked up at me, her face sadder than I had ever seen her look. Obviously, she must have been reading through my father's old letters, the streaks on her cheeks and her red eyes gave her away. She must have been crying about the good times.

'Mum,' I cried. I knelt down on the floor beside her and we hugged for a long time. It had been ages since I had just hugged my mother. Her warmth gave me strength and I said, 'Come on, let's put these away, shall we?'

She nodded, but did not make a move. So, I started to gather up the papers and put them away into the box which lay by her side.

My mother was still sad, as if the sadness was pushing her down and not letting her move.

'There,' I said. 'Let's take you downstairs for a cup of tea.' Seeing her like this had made me forget my own problems, if only for a second. She had lost her husband after all. I helped her to her feet, but then noticed that she was still holding a letter. I took it and was just about to put it away when I saw my name written at the top. Suddenly, my mother snapped out of her daze. 'Eva?' she said. Then she noticed that I had begun to read the letter.

'No, Eva!' my mother said. But it was too late. I had already read it.

'My Darling Eva,

Before you read any further, you should know that your mother and I love you very much. She doesn't want me to write this letter, because she loves you and wants to protect you. That's all she has ever wanted - that's how fiercely protective she is of you. But I love you so much that I have to write it. I sit here wrestling to find the words to say to you. I knew the day would come when you had to know the truth.

Many years ago, I met a wonderful young lady during one of my visits to my aunt's house. The young lady had been taken in by my aunt and uncle as she was found wandering the streets of Portsmouth. She was pregnant and alone. As soon as I saw her, I knew she was the one. You should have seen her, Eva, as she was. So young, so full of life.

I moved her out of my aunt's house and

took her back to London with me. Even though I lived in a small bedsit, life was wonderful for us. We got married as soon as we could and not long after, you were born.

For me, everything changed the moment I saw you. At that moment, the space in my heart was filled. You were our little girl, Evelyn Abigail Johnson. How could you know how much joy you brought us? Even though you are not my by blood, Eva, you're mine in every other way.

I love you darling always and forever,

DADDY'

Horrified, I gasped.

Fresh tears had followed the tracks down my mother's face.

'No, Eva, please believe me when I say, it's not what you think.'

I opened my mouth, but no words came out. Suddenly, I could not stand it any longer. I felt like I was suffocating. It was all too much. For the second time that day, I felt that I needed to get away. I had come here for comfort, for solace, instead, what had I found?

I had no choice but to run. It was not a conscious decision, it just happened. One minute I was holding the letter and the next I found myself running down the street.

I arrived back home to find Richard's car parked outside. Great!

Richard was in the living room, his face had a look of concern.

'Don't talk to me, Richard,' I warned.

'Eva, look, it's not what you think.'

He looked devastated. But my head was whirring. In my mind, all I could see was that smile he gave, just before he saw me. How could he? He was talking, but I could not hear him. Just making some flimsy excuse. What could he say after I had seen him with my own eyes?

I walked through into the kitchen. Richard followed.

'Baby, please, you've got to believe me...' Just empty words. I was standing at the window, staring out at the garden, thinking about the great times we had had in there. How often I had planned to spend long lazy afternoons with my kids out here. So many hopes and dreams, shattered. Richard was still speaking. Why was he here? What did he want from me?

'Baby,' I felt his touch on my arm and it made my skin crawl.

'Don't touch me!' I warned.

'But, honey…'

I felt a rage welling up inside me. Words from my father's letter swam before my eyes: 'Even though you are not my blood.' I felt an anger that I had never felt before. A redness seemed to fill the room and in the middle of it, Richard's face floated like a ghoul. That bastard had the nerve to follow me into our home and plead with me.

Blindly I found that I was clutching something cold and hard in my hands. Richard was still talking.

'Shut up!' I yelled. I stabbed at him with the object.

'Stop talking!'

He looked at me, suddenly stunned. His face looked like a stupid huge fish, floating there in the redness, eyes wide and mouth gaping. No words came out of that lying mouth anymore. He clutched his chest and his hands came away red and sticky. He looked at his hands in disbelief as his mouth filled up with blood too and he collapsed onto the floor. I stood nearby, stunned.

At the back of my mind I was aware of the doorbell ringing, as if I was in another world. I didn't move, but a mad laugh escaped from my lips, suddenly and unexpectedly. They can't see us like this.

Whoever it is can just go away. But it was too late. I heard a strangled scream and then my sister ran to my side.

'Eva!' She checked me over and then screamed again as she noticed the knife in my hand. I did not move. I could not face the scene again. Staring blankly at the garden, I was lost.

'Mum!'

I heard them bustling with activity around me. Janet screamed for a cloth and held it hard against Richard's chest. I heard my mother dial for an ambulance.

'…There's been an accident, please come quickly…'

'Hm!' An accident, I thought.

'Eva?' Someone had come in with them. I felt a touch on my arm.

'Eva!'

A part of my mind reeled and I came to, as if waking up from the worst nightmare. I turned around to come face to face with the last person I wanted to see; 'J'.

'Get away from me!'

My hand twitched and I realised that I was still holding the knife. With a scream, I lunged out but it was no use. The paramedics were already here. They quickly restrained me. I felt something being tied around my arms and the knife was taken away.

Nearby, Richard's body still lay, surrounded by a dark pool. Someone was kneeling by him, listening to his chest. But before I knew it, I felt the rush of a cold liquid starting to flow into my arm and everything began to grow dark.

The voices of the paramedics began to fade away as consciousness fled. I struggled to hold on. To tell them why. I had to explain. They strapped me to a stretcher.

'No! Please listen,' I whispered. 'I will never accept this.'